About the author

Jean Illingworth lives in North Yorkshire with her husband, DJ, and son, Jamie. She has written several books for children, co-written and illustrated by Jamie, but this is her first standalone children's book. When not writing, Jean enjoys photographing the stunning Yorkshire coast and countryside, is a passionate gardener, and enjoys singing and socialising with family and friends.

TWO DEGREES

JEAN ILLINGWORTH

TWO DEGREES

Vanguard Press

A CIP catalogue record for this title is
available from the British Library.

ISBN 978 1 80016 200 6

Vanguard Press is an imprint of
Pegasus Elliot MacKenzie Publishers Ltd.
www.pegasuspublishers.com

First Published in 2021

Vanguard Press
Sheraton House Castle Park
Cambridge England

Printed & Bound in Great Britain

Dedication

Dedicated to all tomorrow's children to whom we hand, with apologies, the fight for the future of our planet.

Acknowledgements

With love and thanks to my husband, DJ, for giving me the space to write and for endless proofreading and cups of tea.

Thank you also to my talented son, Jamie, who usually co-writes and illustrates my books — it's not half as much fun writing on my own!

Thank you to my dear sister, Dorothy Galilee, for being the first to read it and give honest feedback.

Thank you to my colleagues at beautiful St Peter's School, York, for putting up with me wittering on about this book, and for 'lending' me the school as a location at the beginning of the book. Fingers crossed what I have prophesised doesn't come true!

Finally, thank you to Greta Thunberg for having the courage to stand up for her generation's future and for giving me the inspiration for this book.

Chapter One
York, North Yorkshire 2039

The siren woke Lexey from a deep sleep, but she was instantly awake and pulling her clothes on, knowing exactly what the sound meant. Her mother had told her that it was a World War Two air raid siren, but as that was nearly a century before Lexey was born she didn't know if that was true or not. They were facing a war of a different type now, fighting an enemy of their own creation in a battle they could never win, all they could hope for was to survive.

Lexey looked out the window and could see that the water had long since breached the first flood wall at the end of the street and was already flowing over their reinforced garden wall. Thankfully, the metal shutters were firmly in place across the downstairs windows, as the dinghy, that by law they had kept on their front lawn, was already slowly floating up past them.

Calling to her mother, Lexey attached the rope ladder to its bracket on her windowsill and threw the other end into the boat. By the time she'd done that, her mother, Sarah, had appeared clutching a large waterproof holdall.

"Have you got your bag?" asked Sarah.

Lexey nodded and pulled her own bag out from under her bed before tying a rope to the bag's handles. She threaded the other end of the rope through a bracket outside the window and then wordlessly handed it to her mother. They had practiced this so often as a drill that she carried out the actions automatically, but still her heart felt like it was beating out of her chest as she climbed down the swinging rope ladder and into the boat. The rain was coming down in sheets, and despite her supposedly waterproof jacket, she was soon soaked to the skin.

"Okay, Mum, lower the bag down now," Lexey called up to her mother.

Sarah did so, and once that was safely in the boat, pulled the rope back up and then lowered the second bag to her daughter. The next bit was more difficult, as Sarah had to stand on the swaying rope ladder whilst trying to close the window and fasten the external metal shutters over it. Lexey held the ladder as still as she could, but with the water rising steadily and the boat bobbing around it still took longer than it had in the practice runs.

By the time Sarah was safely in the boat and they'd picked up the oars, the water was deep enough to row easily over where the garden wall was hidden under the muddy, swirling water. Joining other boats all moving in one direction above the roadway, they rowed until the water became too shallow and they had almost reached the next flood wall.

Lexey and Sarah jumped out and splashed through the last few feet of water, pulling the dinghy behind them. They retrieved their bags from the boat and handed the tethering rope to an official who asked their names and then ticked them off his list.

Mother and daughter passed through the large metal door in the wall and onto the street on the other side. Although rain was running like a river down the road, there was no flooding yet on this side of the wall, so they were able to make their way fairly easily to their muster point in the main hall of nearby St Peter's School. They were given a towel and a hot drink and shown to two adjacent camp beds amongst those neatly lined up in the school's main hall. Sarah held a towel around Lexey as she peeled off her wet clothes and changed into dry ones from her bag. They repeated this process for Sarah, and then the two sat side by side on one bed and looked around the elegant hall.

"Do you remember coming her once?" Sarah asked her daughter.

Lexey nodded and grinned at her mum.

"I've never forgotten, even though I was only three. It was the school's fourteen-hundredth birthday celebration and I think that all of York came to see the king unveil a plaque. The food and fireworks were amazing, and there was wonderful music. I thought it was a magical place and I *so* wanted to come to school here."

There was a moment's silence as they remembered that happy day before everything went wrong.

"You should have come here, darling," said Sarah sadly. "As soon as you were born we put your name down to start at St Peter's when you were eight."

"You did?" exclaimed Lexey. "What happened, why didn't I come here?"

"This happened," said Sarah, indicating with a sweep of her hand the wet neighbours streaming into the hall. "The primary school was at the bottom of the school's campus, near the River Ouse," she continued. "In 2021, three years before you were born, the Environment Agency increased the height of the flood defences between the school and the river, protecting it from flooding. However, by the time you were three and visited here, the flood defences were regularly being breached and the school was often flooded. By the time you were eight and should have started at the school, the primary school was closed. So far, the senior school has escaped flooding, but I don't know for how much longer."

Sarah shook her head sadly, and Lexey suggested they have a walk around the school to remind them of a happier day. They sat for a little while in the still, silent space of the beautiful chapel and then looked at the names of headmasters and illustrious old pupils carved into oak boards hanging above stone flagged hallways. It would be sad to lose all this history, but then too many wonderful buildings had already been lost in York to worry too much about one more.

Lexey couldn't help thinking about how different her education and her life would have been if global warming had been prevented. At her age, her parent's goals had been to study hard and get to university, but now learning to survive in a rapidly changing world was much more important.

She remembered being taught at school about Greta Thunberg, a brave girl who, at the same age Lexey was now, inspired school children to strike for climate change and accused politicians worldwide of selling their children's future. They mocked her and didn't listen, but once global warming had exceeded 1.5 degrees centigrade, it was too late to stop it, and drought, floods, extreme heat and devastating fires became the new norm.

The Americans tried geoengineering, firing sulphate aerosols into the stratosphere to reflect sunlight back to space. At first, this seemed to work, and temperatures started to drop, but then the chemicals caused the almost mended hole in the ozone layer to grow and the temperature to rise again. The chemicals made rain more acidic, causing some crops to fail, so before long the technology was outlawed. Global warming spiralled rapidly, and in a shockingly short period of time it was at 2 degrees centigrade. Whole areas of the world were becoming uninhabitable, with fertile land turning to desert and raging fires devastating what was left of the forests. Many parts of the world were affected by famine and food scarcity, and several species of animals and insects had been lost forever.

In the UK, the deflection of the Gulf Stream had meant that it hadn't become significantly hotter, just much, much wetter, with almost constant heavy rain that sapped everyone's spirits. Melting glaciers had caused rising sea levels and many coastal communities had already been lost to the sea. Now flooding was threatening to destroy many inland regions as well. Sunny carefree days were a distant memory for Lexey, and she sighed and took her mum's hand.

"What do we do now, Mum?" she asked.

Sarah took her mobile phone from her pocket and looked at the screen. No signal as usual. She didn't know why she still carried it around as the mobile network had long since crashed. No one really knew why, but some thought it was the increased solar radiation which now brought almost nightly aurora borealis to UK skies, and some thought it was lack of maintenance of transmitters in flooded areas. Others thought it was the government deliberately blocking it to stop civil unrest spreading, especially as the internet also barely functioned any more.

"I'm going to see if I can borrow a landline phone and ring your Auntie Jenny," said Sarah. "She's high up on the North Yorkshire moors where it's very unlikely to ever flood. How about you go and stay with her a while? I know she could do with the help."

"What about you, Mum?" replied Lexey. "I don't want to go without you!"

"I need to stay here, darling, and see what I can salvage from the house if the water recedes," said Sarah quietly.

"That doesn't matter, Mum, I'm sure Auntie Jenny has everything we could possibly need," replied Lexey, grabbing her mum's hand again. "I've lost Dad, and I don't want to lose you too!"

"Your dad's not lost, darling, and the main reason I need to stay here is to be here when he gets back."

"Mum, we haven't heard from him for two months! I know he had to go to Spain on business, but why hasn't he come home and why haven't we heard from him?"

"I don't know, darling, all I know is that he had to go, and he said he would be back as soon as he could. Your dad is a survivor, and if he said he was coming back, he will, even if it takes him a while. I'm going to stay here and wait from him, and then we'll both come and join you and Jenny."

Sarah gave Lexey's hand a squeeze and then went to see if she could use a landline phone.

Chapter Two

Aunt Jenny's ancient Land Rover pulling up outside the school caused quite a stir. Vehicles powered by fossil fuels were almost universally banned, electric or solar powered vehicles being the usual means of transport, but in York, cycles, scooters and in some areas, boats, were much more usual.

Farmers had a special dispensation, but the fuel was supposed to be used for tractors, so Aunt Jenny had probably broken a lot of rules to come for her niece. Not that she cared. Jenny had stopped caring about what anyone thought the day her husband had died. But she did care about her sister and niece, so when Sarah had rung her, she had set off to fetch Lexey without a second's hesitation.

Jenny hugged her sister warmly and they talked for minute, their arms tight around each other. Lexey hung back, trying to hear what they were saying, but from her mum's stubborn expression she thought maybe Jenny was trying to persuade her to come too. Jenny gave an exasperated sigh and then turned and hugged Lexey before picking up her bag and dashing through the rain with it to the car. Lexey clung to her mother for a long time before Jenny parped her horn.

"Come on, Lexey, we need to get back before its dark," she shouted. "Say goodbye to your mother — you'll see her again very soon."

Lexey didn't believe that for a moment, but after urging her mum to take great care, she ran to the car and reluctantly climbed in. Jenny didn't know if it was rain on Lexey's face or tears, but she silently handed her a tissue and put the old car into gear.

Getting out of York required a few detours to avoid flooded areas, but soon they were speeding through narrow, winding country lanes, sending great arcs of water up over the already sodden hedges.

Jenny sped on, taking bends far too fast for Lexey's liking, and she tightened her seat belt further. Jenny noticed and laughed, before slowing down slightly as they entered a small village on top of a hill. There was no flooding here, and Lexey looked longingly at the picturesque stone cottages with flowers and vegetables growing in their gardens. The rain had eased, and neighbours stood chatting in front of an ancient church as if they hadn't a care in the world.

The next village was very different; nestled in a dip in the road, many of its houses and gardens were partly under water and there was not a soul about. Jenny slowed right down to cross the lake that had formed on the road, the water coming up to the door sills. Once they were out the other side, she tested her brakes before powering on in the gloom between the high hedges and dripping trees. It started to rain heavily again, and even with the wipers on double speed, visibility was poor. To allow her aunt to concentrate, Lexey sat in silence, clinging to the sides of her seat as they careered around bends and skidded on the surface water.

They reached the market town of Helmsley without mishap, but crossing the narrow, curving bridge into the town was going to be difficult as it was flooded almost to its parapet. The shops and cottages nearest to the previously narrow River Rye were already partly flooded, and those higher up had sandbags across their doors. Jenny pulled up just before the bridge and leaned out of the window to appraise the situation.

"Hmm, this is a lot worse than earlier," muttered Jenny. "Undo your seatbelt, Lexey, and wind your window down. If we go over into the river, you'll need to be able to get out through the window immediately and swim to the bank.

"Wha…" exclaimed Lexey. "Can't we go around?"

"It would be a very long detour, and no guarantee other parts won't be worse, plus it will be dark soon, so, hang on, we're going through," replied Jenny, shifting the old Land Rover into gear.

With no time to panic, Lexey unclipped her seatbelt, wound the window down as instructed and then leaned over to undo her aunt's seatbelt too. They edged cautiously forward, the water halfway up the door and seeping into the footwell. The vehicle continued to creep forward, its wheels still in contact with the road, but at the bend in the bridge it started to drift, scraping along the bridge parapet with an awful keening sound.

The vehicle started to tilt and Lexey bit back a scream, willing the car not to turn over and fall into the raging river.

"Lean the other way!" shouted her aunt, and Lexey threw her weight against the door as instructed.

Then, miraculously, the wheels found the road again and they suddenly shot out the other side of the bridge, before coming to a shuddering halt a little further up in the relatively dry old market square.

"Well, that was fun," said Jenny, wryly.

Lexey, struggling to get her breathing under control, said nothing, just glared at her aunt.

"We may not be able to get into town again soon, so I'll stock up on supplies here," said Jenny, climbing out of the car and stretching the kinks out of her back.

Lexey climbed down and followed her aunt through the rain to the little supermarket that nestled amongst the gift shops and cafés of the quaint tourist town. The shelves were pretty empty, but Jenny filled a couple of baskets with what there was, candles, matches, toilet paper, bags of flour, dried yeast, cocoa, blocks of margarine, a variety of tins and a bottle of whisky. Lexey added in shampoo and several bars of chocolate and, at the last minute, grabbed a newspaper.

After about another half hour of driving on roads that got steadily narrower, and just as darkness was falling, they arrived at Aunt Jenny's farm, high up on the edge of the moors. The farmyard was a quagmire, but Jenny seemed unconcerned at the mud they tramped onto the stone floors of her old kitchen. Not giving Lexey time to unpack or put on dry clothes, Jenny sent her straight out to feed and lock up the chickens whilst she fed the pigs and goats.

Feeding the chickens used to be Lexey's favourite task when she had spent summers on the farm as a small child, but tired, sad, wet and cold it was much less fun, especially as the old rooster contrived to elude her. However, when she eventually squelched back into the kitchen, she was greeted by the warmth of the range and a bowl of hot soup, which restored her usual good temper a little.

Chapter Three
North Yorkshire Moors 2039

The next day it was not raining, but was hot and humid, with steam coming off the mud and damp vegetation. Lexey helped her aunt around the farm, noting the changes since her Uncle Andrew had died. She had never been told how he died; all she knew was that he had been found dead in his tractor in the middle of a field of corn. With the constant rain, their corn had not ripened and had just rotted on the stalk, which had been a big financial loss for them. Lexey couldn't help wondering if her uncle had committed suicide, especially as her aunt's moods veered between sadness and anger, but she had never dared ask.

Since her husband's death, Auntie Jenny had rented off the arable fields and sold her dairy herd, just keeping a few pigs, a lot of free-range chickens and several goats. Wandering around the farm Lexey noted that her aunt was growing lots of different vegetables in raised mounds. There were spring onions, spinach and artichokes but most of the others she didn't recognise, and assumed her aunt was trying out new varieties that liked wet weather. There was also rhubarb, gooseberries, jostaberries and currants which seemed to be doing well, and the orchard had been extended with new pear trees and different varieties of apples, some of which were doing better than others.

Lexey was impressed at her aunt's changes around the farm, but less so with the interior of the old farmhouse, which looked like it hadn't been cleaned for months. Over the next few days, between feeding the chickens, pigs and goats, collecting eggs and weeding vegetables, Lexey made it her mission to clean the farmhouse, room by room. This was partly to help her aunt but mainly because keeping busy didn't give her time to worry about her mum and dad.

It was whilst cleaning her aunt's bedroom that she found the key to the gun locker. Uncle Andrew had regularly taken groups of businessmen grouse shooting in season and had a selection of fine guns that were always kept securely locked up. As a small child, Lexey had loved the excitement of the shooting parties, the men — dressed in tweeds and hats like something out of an old film — setting off amongst much noise and laughter with their guns broken over their arms. Aunt Jenny would cook a wonderful supper for the huntsmen's triumphant return, but although Lexey wasn't allowed to join them, there would be plenty of leftovers to enjoy the next day.

Five years ago, the burning of the moorland heather, done to encourage the new shoots that the grouse fed on, was banned, and that was the end of the shooting parties. Lexey understood why the ban had come in, as any large scale burning added to global warming, and the denuded hillside allowed heavy rain to run straight down into the valleys below causing flooding. However, she also could see the impact the ban had had on her aunt and uncle as the hunting parties had brought a lot of much needed money to the farm.

The gun locker key was in an old mug on her uncle's side of the bed. Lexey recognised it instantly as it had a green tassel attached which hung limply outside of the cup. She picked it up and sat down on the bed, holding it in her hand, remembering a day long ago when the key had gone missing and Lexey had found it for her uncle. As a reward he had borrowed a pony from a neighbouring farm for her to ride. The pony probably had a name of its own, but Lexey had called it Beauty, and that summer, learning to ride and care for Beauty, had been one of the happiest of her life.

Remembering her uncle's kindness brought a tear to Lexey's eye. She wiped it away with the back of her hand and put the key back, noticing that her uncle's glasses, and a book with a bookmark halfway through, were still on the bedside table. Lexey thought this was a bit creepy, but even more so were her uncle's clothes still hanging in the wardrobe. They gave off a faint whiff of her uncle, a mixture of soap, farmyard and well, just him, which made her cry in earnest.

Lexey abandoned the bedroom and tackled the bathroom instead, taking her sadness and frustration out on the grime. Whilst cleaning the mirror on the bathroom cabinet she stopped and stared at her reflection. Her long, light brown hair hung limply like curtains either side of her pale face and her freckles stood out starkly across her nose. Her fringe was too long, getting into her eyes, and she toyed with the idea of growing it out, before taking the nail scissors from the cabinet and hacking chunks off it. Although uneven, it emphasised her deep brown eyes and she realised with a bit of a shock she hadn't worn mascara for ages.

With more important things to think about, her generation focused far less on appearance than her parents and grandparents, and the vacuous taking of endless selfies was a thing of the past. Before the internet crashed, most young people's social media posts had been about climate change, and the anger started by her parent's generation in the Extinction Rebellion had become an all-encompassing passion sweeping away the culture of celebrities and other frivolous obsessions.

Lexey cleared up the hair and then cleaned the sink and the bath. The environmentally friendly cleaner her aunt used did little to remove the ring around the toilet, but the rest of the bathroom looked much fresher and Lexey felt a bit happier knowing she had achieved something.

Over the next few days, her aunt taught her to milk the goats and make goats' cheese. Goats' milk on cereal was an acquired taste, but with nothing else, Lexey got used to it. Jenny also taught her how to make bread, and

Lexey loved the whole process of kneading and shaping the dough, letting it rise and then knocking it back before allowing it to rise again. She loved the silky feel of the dough and the yeasty smell, and especially the wonderful aroma as it baked in the range.

Keeping busy made the first week pass quickly, but Lexey was getting gradually more anxious about her mum and dad as time passed with no news. She had tried phoning their home number, but just got the number unobtainable tone. Jenny had tried phoning the school that had been used as a refuge, but the phone just rang out unanswered. It was a bit of a shock, therefore, when the phone suddenly rang in the kitchen one evening whilst they sat reading by the range. They both jumped, and Jenny put her hand to her chest before leaping up and grabbing the phone, almost dropping it in her haste.

"Hello," Jenny said, uncertainly.

Lexey knew instantly it was her mum as a look of relief flooded her aunt's face and she grabbed the phone off her.

"Mum!" she shouted. "Are you okay?"

"Hello, darling, I'm fine. Are you oaky?" asked her mum.

"I'm great, Mum, but missing you. When will you be here?" replied Lexey.

"Well, that's what I'm ringing about. If you put your aunt back on, we'll see what we can sort out."

Lexey reluctantly handed the phone to Jenny and hovered at her elbow, waiting to get it back to find out what her mum had been doing and if there was any news of her dad. Jenny glanced at Lexey and then took the phone into the other room and closed the door. When she returned to the kitchen, she put the phone back in the charger without giving it to Lexey.

"Oh, Aunt, I wanted to speak to her!" cried Lexey petulantly.

"I know, love, sorry, but she was borrowing the phone and couldn't stay on. There is something I need to help her with first, but you'll see her very soon and she can tell you everything face to face," replied Jenny, soothingly. "How about you go lock up the chickens, and we have an early night, and then I can be up early tomorrow to get to York to help your mum?"

Chapter Four

When Lexey woke the next morning, her aunt had already left, and the house felt strangely quiet. She busied herself feeding the animals and collecting the eggs, and then set about baking some bread to welcome her mum. Whilst that was rising, she decided to attempt to bake a cake as well, something she used to do regularly with her mother when she was little. The smell of baking filled the kitchen and Lexey put the radio on and hummed as she worked, enjoying playing house.

The radio was an old-fashioned DAB radio, not the normal smart speaker everyone had, and was tuned to some oldies channel playing turn of the century music. She recognised many of the songs as ones her mother used to play on her guitar, singing along in her lovely rich voice at family gatherings, with her father joining in with improvised harmonies. Lexey had loved it when she was little and would get up and do her own party piece, but had been mortified as a teenager when her mum got the guitar out in front of her school friends.

'What I wouldn't give to hear my mum and dad singing together now,' Lexey thought sadly.

Sitting down for a cup of tea whilst the cake was cooking, Lexey spied the paper she'd bought the week before but had just left on the dresser, unread. She flicked through it idly but then an article leapt out at her, causing her to gasp out loud. It was a report on conditions in Europe and talked about extreme heat and fires in Spain. It said that all airports were closed as the runways had melted. No wonder her dad hadn't been able to get home! Lexey's good mood evaporated, and she just wanted her mum to arrive and tell her everything would be okay.

She listened carefully to the news on the radio to see if there was any mention of road conditions or flooding in North Yorkshire, but there was very little news at all; maybe because there were just too many problems everywhere to condense into two minutes. The weather forecast was, once again, for rain, with a warning of a severe storm in the next day or two. Like most people nowadays, Aunt Jenny didn't have a TV, so Lexey switched on her aunt's old laptop in the hope of getting more information. She hadn't much hope of the internet miraculously working today, but she didn't have the chance to find out as there was no connection at all. Whether there wasn't any wi-fi at the farm, or whether it was just down at present, Lexey didn't know, but it added to her sense of despondency.

Once midday had passed and the afternoon wore on, Lexey began to get more anxious. 'Surely, they should have been back by now?' she thought.

'Let me see,' she said to herself. 'The journey into York should normally take about one and a half hours, two if the roads were bad. Maybe three if they had to do a detour? So, the round trip would be six hours, tops.'

She nodded to herself and glanced at the kitchen clock which was showing nearly four p.m.; if Aunt Jenny had set off before seven a.m. as she must have done, she'd been gone at least nine hours.

Lexey felt increasingly anxious: she was no longer enjoying being home alone. She went to the door and looked out. The constant rain of the last two days had eased to a drizzle, and unable to wait any longer, Lexey decided to walk down the road a mile or so to where there was a view over the valley and see if she could spot any approaching vehicles.

She wondered if she ought to change her old trainers for a pair of her aunt's walking boots, but was eager to get going, so just pulled on one of her aunt's old coats and set off down the track. Once she was off the farm, the moors opened up on either side of her, heather and bracken dripping with rain as far as she could see. The drizzle gradually stopped, and a watery sunshine brought a little colour back to the muted palette of greens and rusts. The sun lifted her spirits a little as she left the road and picked her way between tussocks of grass and boggy areas to reach a rocky outcrop where in spring a mass of foxgloves would paint the hillside a vibrant magenta.

Lexey climbed nimbly up onto the rocks and looked out across the valley and found herself temporarily dazzled by sunlight reflected off water. She shaded her eyes against the glare of sunlight and her mouth fell open in shock. Every dip and hollow of the moors were a pool of silver, and the only road disappeared into a shimmering lake in the valley far below. There was not a single vehicle on the road and, apart from a flock of white birds that glided in and landed on the lake, there was no movement anywhere.

Lexey sat down on the rock and just stared at the view as the afternoon faded to evening and the setting sun met the lake, turning it to fire. She remained sitting there, in despair and utterly alone, as the stars came out and the green fingers of the aurora danced across the sky. This brought her back to herself a little, and she stared at it in wonder. She had seen it many times before, but here in the middle of nowhere with no light pollution, it was mesmerising, its colours and patterns more intense than she had ever seen before. Curtains of luminous green hung high in the sky, dipping and swaying, melting into carmine and acid yellow and then back to vivid green.

Lexey remembered when, as a little girl, she had first seen a vivid aurora in the sky above York. Her mum told her that pale wisps of green light had been seen locally a few times before, but never anything as clear and vibrant. All around her people stopped in the street and stared, recording it on their phones and clapping when new colours appeared. Lexey had held tight to her mum and dad's hands, excited not just at the light show but at staying up so late on a school night. Her dad had tried to explain to her what the aurora borealis was, but she wasn't listening — it was just magic as far as she was concerned.

Stunning auroras had soon become as common as a rainbow in the sky above York and before long people stopped taking any notice of it. In fact, mused Lexey, rainbows were probably less common as that required sunshine as well as rain and that was a rare commodity nowadays.

Lexey lay back on the rock and looked up at the stars. There were so many of them, many more than she'd ever been able to see in the city. She looked for the Plough and the North Star as her father had taught her and wondered if he was looking at them too. She missed him dreadfully and felt so small and lost under the infinite space above her. She felt like the weight of the universe was pressing down on her chest and panic started to rise up inside her, a kind of agoraphobia brought on by the vastness of her surroundings.

Lexey sat up and tried to slow her breathing down. She was shivering and realising how cold she had become and how dark the moors were around her. She carefully eased herself down from the rock, and, wishing she had a torch, made her way blindly across the moor. She hadn't gone far before her foot slipped off a tussock and she fell forward, landing face down in the mud. Her foot was stuck behind her, wedged in the gap between grass mounds and twisted at an abnormal angle. The pain was instant, and she yelled out loud, disturbing roosting birds that flapped up squawking around her, causing her heart to start racing again.

Lexey wiped mud from her eyes and nose before freeing her ankle by manually lifting her leg out of the gap, but when she tried to stand up, her ankle wouldn't support her. The stabbing pain brought tears to her eyes and she fumbled in the coat pocket for a tissue. Her fingers found something else, and she realised with a jolt of hope that it was her aunt's mobile phone. Pulling it out carefully, terrified of dropping it into the mud, she turned it on, and the screen flared into life.

There was no phone signal at all, and she hadn't expected there would be, but she found the torch function and its welcome light beamed out, giving her hope. Shining it all around she could see she was a long way from the road and crawling over the bumpy, waterlogged moors to it would be almost impossible. Close by, however, she spotted an old shooting hide made of local stone and topped with growing heather to disguise it. That would at least give her some shelter, and having no other option, she hopped and stumbled towards it, dragging her leg painfully behind her.

Inside the shelter of the hide it was marginally warmer and the ground was smooth and level, so Lexey thought she'd rest there for a little while, then try again to get back to the farmhouse. She curled up into a foetal position on the ground, her back against the rough stone wall, and fell immediately into an exhausted sleep.

Heavy rain woke her just as dawn started to lighten the sky, and she sat up with a start, completely disorientated. Her whole body was stiff and sore from sleeping on the damp ground and her ankle throbbed painfully. She rolled down her sock and looked at her ankle and, even in the dim dawn light, she could see it was hugely swollen and turning black. Cautiously she moved her toes and then moved her foot from side to side slightly. It was very painful, but she was relieved to find she had some movement which suggested it was sprained rather than broken.

She took off her aunt's coat and then removed her tee-shirt, putting the coat back on quickly over her bra. With some difficulty she ripped the tee-shirt into broad strips and then used these to bind her ankle tightly. Taking a deep breath and holding onto the stones of the hide, she pulled herself upright on her good leg. Gingerly she put a little weight onto her bad leg, and although very painful, it didn't give way.

Lexey looked around for something to use as a crutch and her eyes fell on a plank extending across the hide which was intended for resting guns on. This was wedged into the stones on either side but she soon yanked it free from the crumbling structure. It was the perfect length although too wide to hold in one hand, but by holding it in both hands and planting it in front of her she was able to hobble forward one slow step at a time.

Once on the smooth road it was easier, but still painful and slow. She heard the vehicle before she saw it, coming towards her at speed, and just had time to limp to the side of the road before it shot past, the driver ignoring her frantic waving. However, it wasn't long before it was back, having reached the lake and, unable to get any further, turned around. This time it slowed as it approached her and then stopped. It was on old black pickup truck, much dented and splattered with mud, and inside were two young men, farmhands by the looks of them. The driver, a man of about twenty-five with a scruffy beard, leaned out of the window and looked Lexey up and down in a way that made her feel very uncomfortable. She felt helpless due to her injury, and was aware she must look a sight, her clothes crumpled and covered in mud, her hair a wild mess.

"Hi, love, what are you doing out here?" asked the driver in a north-east accent.

"Going for a walk," replied Lexey, turning away from them and hobbling off.

"Oh yeah?" said the other one, who looked a bit older and had thinning hair tied back in a ponytail. "Well, you're not going to get very far like that are you. Hop in and we'll give you a lift," he continued.

"Hop in!" repeated the driver. "That's good, Shaun, looks like all she *can* do is hop!" They both laughed uproariously as if it was the funniest thing in the world.

Lexey didn't know what to do. She didn't like the look of them and knew it was foolish to get into a car with strange men, but on the other hand, it was going to take her hours to get home on her own. She was also very conscious that she only had her bra on under her coat which made her feel especially vulnerable. In the end, the decision was not really hers, as Shaun got out and took her arm, propelling her into the car.

"Where too?" the driver asked, and Lexey directed them towards the farm.

"You here all on your own then?" asked Shaun.

"No, no," lied Lexey. "My mum, dad and aunt are here too."

Shaun just grunted, and nothing else was said until they reached the farmhouse.

"Nice place," said the driver, looking around the farmyard appraisingly.

"Thank you," said Lexey climbing out immediately and limping as fast as she could towards the door. "And thank you for the lift."

"Aren't you going to ask us in?" called Shaun.

"Sorry, not today." replied Lexey. "My dad's got 'flu and I wouldn't want you to catch it."

She quickly went inside and locked the door behind her, leaning against it until she heard them drive off. She waited a few more moments to make sure, and then limped outside to see to the animals. She had thought things couldn't get worse and was unprepared for the scene of devastation awaiting her at the back of the farmhouse. The yard was splattered with blood and chicken feathers, and the remains of several dismembered birds were scattered around.

"Oh no, no," sobbed Lexey, realising immediately that as she hadn't been back last night to lock up the chickens, a fox had got them.

She saw the head of her favourite chicken, Lucky, discarded in a puddle, and sat down on the back step, put her head in her hands and cried. Then a blur of movement caught her attention, and she looked up to see the rooster, followed by several of his ladies, strutting across the yard towards her in search of corn. They must have hidden somewhere and escaped the attack, and Lexey gave a sigh of relief that not all were lost.

Lexey found an old walking stick in a pot in the hall and her priority was then to make sure all the animals were fed, the goats milked, and the remaining chickens shut up safely. Once done, she hauled her exhausted and dirty body upstairs and lay in a hot bath until it was almost cold. She put on a pair of her aunt's flannelette pyjamas, crawled into bed, and fell instantly asleep.

Chapter Five

It was the middle of the afternoon when Lexey woke up, feeling disorientated and on edge. Her ankle was still very painful, but a bit easier once she had wrapped it in a crêpe bandage from her aunt's first aid box. Her stomach rumbled, and she realised she hadn't eaten since the previous day's lunch, but one look outside at the remains of dead chickens spread across the yard put her off eating. She hobbled outside and found a shovel and a bucket and scooped the remains up. She didn't know whether to put them in the bin, bury them or feed them to the pigs. In the end she fed them to the pigs as the most environmentally friendly option, even though doing so turned her stomach further.

Lexey wondered if she should scrub the yard clean, but seeing the looming black thunder clouds made her realise that wouldn't be necessary. She checked on the pigs and goats and then fed the chickens again, double checking that the fences and gates were secure, before rushing inside ahead of the approaching storm. It was almost as dark as night in the kitchen, and she hurriedly flicked the lights on. That made things a little more cheerful but as the first crash of thunder rattled the windows, Lexey started to shiver. She went to lean on the range rail for some comforting warmth but found to her dismay it had gone out. She knew she should relight it and then eat something, but just didn't seem to have the energy.

Aunt Jenny's old cardigan was draped around a kitchen chair and Lexey pulled it on, hugging it tight around herself. She stood there uncertain, unable to decide whether to just go back to bed or make something to eat, but then her stomach rumbled again and that decided it for her.

'Soup,' she said to herself, 'that's quick and warming.'

Lexey found a tin of tomato soup in the pantry and emptied it into a bowl, putting it into the microwave to heat up quickly. She glanced at the loaf of bread she had made yesterday which was still on the cooling rack where she'd left it, and her eyes filled with tears, remembering she'd made it to welcome her mum. Having decided she would make another loaf tomorrow, as surely her mum would be here by then, she cut herself a thick slice and carried it to the table with the steaming bowl of soup. She added a chunk of cheese from the fridge and an apple from the fruit bowl and smiled at how simple it was to make a more or less balanced meal.

However, before she had taken one mouthful, there was a blinding flash of lightning and simultaneous thunder that sounded like a bomb exploding. The whole house shook, plates rattled on the dresser and she was plunged into darkness.

She dropped the spoon into the soup, and it splashed across her hand, scalding her. Lexey felt her way to the sink and ran cold water over her hand, and then felt for where she'd put her aunt's phone on charge. Switching on the torch function, she went in search of the trip switches. It wasn't something she had ever looked for before, but at home it was under the stairs, so she assumed it would be the same here. Sadly, that was not the case, but she eventually found it high up the wall in the hallway.

Lexey dragged a chair into the hall, and mindful that if she fell and hurt herself badly there was no one to help her, she put the chair against the wall so it wouldn't slip. Climbing onto it with her bad ankle was not easy, but she put her weight onto her good leg as much as possible and held onto the chair back. She knew what she was looking at inside the box, as her dad had made sure she was fairly self-sufficient in household emergencies, but when she flicked the trip-switch nothing happened. She switched it off and then on again a few times, but still nothing. Realising it must be a general power outage, she carefully climbed down and went in search of the candles she remembered her aunt buying in Helmsley.

Although the storm continued to rage outside, once Lexey had lit a few candles, things looked quite cosy and she returned to her now lukewarm soup, feeling strangely more cheerful. Once she'd eaten, she went in search of a torch and found two along with lots of spare batteries and several more boxes of candles. This suggested that power outages were a regular occurrence at the farm, which gave her hope that the power would be returned before too long.

She knew she ought to relight the range, but she was too cold and tired to make the effort, so, having checked that all the candles were safely out and the doors securely locked, she hobbled her way upstairs by torchlight to the warmth of her bed. The storm continued to rage around the farm, repeatedly filling the room with flashes of searing white light whilst shaking the house with rumbling thunder. If her mum had been there, Lexey would have got into her bed and cuddled up with her, as she always did as a small child during a thunderstorm. Her mum had always made her feel safe, and knowing she now only had herself to rely on was a terrifying thought.

She wondered where her mum and dad were and hoped that they, and Aunt Jenny, were safe and well. She worried about what was keeping them from her, and having had no contact with the outside world for so long, her tired mind began to imagine the worst; an accident, more flooding, war in Europe or a raging disease keeping them quarantined, perhaps?

She remembered her mum telling her about a virus in the twenties that had jumped from animals to humans, causing a pandemic that swept around the world. By the time a vaccine became available to all, millions had died, and economies were starting to crumble.

People had to isolate themselves from others for long periods to slow the spread of the virus, and many became nervous about shopping from big supermarkets and city centre stores. Local shops and farms made home deliveries or set up stalls in the open air, and in the years afterwards, as many people continued to shop locally, regionalisation became more pronounced. Foreign travel was frequently banned to stop new variants coming in from abroad, and due to concerns about the pollution caused by air travel, foreign travel never resumed at the same level as previously. This shift away from centralisation and globalism continued through Lexey's young life, as flooding regularly cut whole areas off for large periods, sometimes forever.

Around the same time, people stopped eating as much meat, partly because the strict new hygiene measures brought in to stop such a plague happening again made it very expensive, and partly because of the knowledge that large scale farming of animals increased global warming.

Lexey remembered studying this period of recent history in spiritualism studies in school. Some Christians had hailed the 'pestilence', along with the more frequent earthquakes and the floods, fires and famine of global warming, as the 'end times' and believed Christ's return was imminent. At the same time, an ancient religion had re-emerged and become very popular, the cult of Gaea, the earth goddess, whose followers believed that the earth was purging itself of human beings, poisoning them with a virus and then cleansing the world with fire and floods.

Lexey believed neither, just that man's greed was to blame. If she had any beliefs, it was in the values that her mum had brought her up with, especially to treat other people as you'd want to be treated yourself. She hoped someone was treating her mum with kindness, wherever she was, and whispered a prayer to a god she didn't believe in that she would come home safely.

Reverting to childhood, Lexey took the torch under a tent of the covers and tried to read a book of her aunt's, but before long she gave up, the racy detective story not holding her attention. She lay rigid for a long time, listening to the storm crash around her, eventually falling into a restless sleep full of vivid nightmares.

***

Lexey was awoken by the sound of car doors banging, jumped straight out of bed and ran to the window, her heart leaping at the hope it was her aunt and mother. The morning light glinted dully off a dirty black pick-up parked in the yard. Shaun was just getting out and making his way to the front door so Lexey shrank back behind the curtains, not wanting him to see her. Shaun hammered on the door and Lexey's heart hammered in her chest. When she didn't answer the door, the driver got out too, and both men walked around the back of the house. Lexey limped across the landing to her aunt's bedroom and watched them from behind the curtain as they banged on the backdoor, and when they got no response, trying the handle.

'Thank goodness I checked it was locked last night,' Lexey thought to herself as she watched the pair turn away.

They appeared to be having a good snoop around, looking at the pigs and goats and examining the fences around the chicken run, and it was some time before she heard them drive off. Lexey let out the breath she didn't realise she was holding and sat down on the edge of her aunt's bed, her shaking legs unable to hold her up any longer. For the first time since being on her own her she felt seriously afraid. Panicked thoughts ran around her head — what did they want? Would they come back? What if her aunt didn't return? How would she survive?

Lexey decide the sensible thing was to call the police. She wished she'd got the pick-up's number plate, but there wouldn't be too many farms around here for the police to track it down. She'd picked up the bedside phone and had dialled 999 before she realised there was no dial tone. She pressed the switch for the bedside lamp; nothing. Realising the power must still be off, she slumped down on the bed, feeling overwhelmed by everything.

However, after a few minutes of wallowing in self-pity, Lexey straightened up, a determined look on her face. She reached over to her late uncle's side of the bed and picked up the green tasselled key.

Chapter Six

Another week passed without Lexey seeing a soul, and apart from the fact that she now kept one loaded shotgun next to her bed and another in the kitchen, nothing else had changed. The power remained off and Lexey's life fell into a routine that must have been very similar to that of the numerous previous generations who had lived in the farmhouse. She fed the animals, milked the goats, collected the eggs and kept the range alight. The spirit-sapping rain returned most days, but thankfully there were no more thunderstorms. A tree had come down in the storm, and as wood for the range was getting low, Lexey cut off the smaller branches with an axe she'd found in a shed, and hacked them into short lengths. She didn't have the strength to cut bigger limbs off the tree, but there was a stack of coal, so she was fine for now.

Her ankle got better day by day, and having found an old bicycle, one dry day she cycled to the viewpoint and climbed up onto the rocks without too much difficulty. There was even more water in the valley than before, and her heart sank, knowing no one could drive through that to get to her. As she cycled despondently back to the farm an idea came to her, and on reaching the farm, she went through her aunt's bookcase and found an old Ordinance Survey Landranger map of the area.

As well as roads, footpaths and rivers, the map showed the topography in faint red ridge lines with heights marked on them. It was obvious why the valley had flooded as it was the lowest point around and was where several small becks met the River Dove. She traced the road past the farm going north rather than going south towards York, and it stayed on high ground right to the edge of the map. Lexey searched the bookcase for the adjacent maps, but there weren't any, so she had no way of knowing if it was possible to get to York by going the opposite direction and then looping round.

Lexey thought about going to a nearby farm for help, but knew most buildings within reasonable distance were just holiday homes and unlikely to be occupied. She was also worried about ending up at the farm of the men with the black pick-up. Her aunt's pantry was very well stocked with basic ingredients and lots of home bottled fruit, and she had daily eggs and goat's milk and could make her own cheese and bread, so she wouldn't starve. Lexey decided it would be better to stay put at present, as her family knew where to find her, and surely the power would come back on soon?

As evening drew in, Lexey lit some candles and curled up with a book in front of the range. Having taken stock and decided to stay where she was, she felt strangely content. She wondered idly what her schoolfriends would be doing and smiled to herself, imagining telling them all about her adventures when she eventually got home. She'd have a bit of catching up to do as it was her Higher Certificate this year, but she was already beginning to wonder what the point of exams was. Fewer and fewer young people seemed to go to university nowadays, either because they didn't want to saddle themselves with the debt, or because academic qualifications were no longer relevant in the rapidly changing world.

Lost in thought, it took Lexey a few minutes to register that the chickens were squawking loudly. She leapt up and grabbed the shotgun, her anger at the fox's return propelling her out the back door into the black night. She sensed rather than saw movement near the gate into the henhouse and pointed the gun in that direction. She had never fired a gun before and hadn't really thought that far ahead. Her hands were shaking, and before she realised how close her finger was to the trigger, her trembling finger slipped, and the gun went off. She was not prepared for the gun's recoil, or for the human sounding scream that instantly filled the air. Lexey landed heavily on her bottom and instinctively put her hands over her ears to block out the continuing scream. She had no idea that a fox could scream like that, but it must be in pain, and she realised that she must put it out of its misery. She felt sick at the thought but made herself run back into the farmhouse for a torch, then advanced slowly, gun in hand, towards the unearthly scream.

Lexey swung the torch beam in an arc and its beam lit up the frightened eyes of, not a fox, but a young man, writhing in pain on the ground.

"Don't shoot!" he screamed, raising his arms in the air. "Please don't shoot!"

"Oh my god!" cried Lexey, putting the gun down and running to the young man. "I'm sorry, I'm so sorry. I thought you were a fox!"

"My leg," sobbed the boy. "You shot me in the leg!"

Lexey directed the torch beam downwards and could see the blood spreading across the lower leg of his jeans. She helped him up onto his good leg and, supporting his weight with his arm around her shoulder, managed to half drag, half carry him into the house. He collapsed into a chair and she stared at him in horror, temporarily paralysed with shock. He wasn't much older than her, a mop of unruly dark hair falling across his face which was etched with pain.

"Help me, please," he said, looking up at her with wide, blue, tear-filled eyes.

Lexey shook herself out of her stupor and dashed to get the first aid kit. Grabbing the kitchen scissors, she cut the leg of his jeans to the knee. It was difficult to see in the candlelight, but only one of the shotgun pellets appeared to have hit him and had gone straight through the side of his calf, gouging a channel of flesh out of the side. There was a lot of blood, and although it was flowing out, it wasn't spurting, so Lexey didn't think she'd hit anything major. Grabbing a large pad, she pressed hard on the wound in an effort to stem the bleeding. The boy swore loudly, but she kept pressing regardless.

"Hold this," she said, when the bleeding had eased a bit.

He did as he was told whilst she filled a clean bowl with boiled water and added antiseptic. She raised the leg up on a stool and bathed it as gently as she could, before applying a clean dressing and binding it tightly.

"Thank goodness I did that first aid course," Lexey said shakily when she had finished.

"I have to go," said the boy, struggling to stand. Immediately blood started to come through the dressing and Lexey pushed him back into the chair.

"You can't," she said firmly.

"I have to," he replied glaring at her. "I've left my little brother alone."

"Your brother? Where?" asked Lexey

"At the cottage. Heather Cottage, about half a mile away," replied the boy.

"I know where Heather Cottage is," replied Lexey. "The O'Connell's old place."

"Yes, my dad, Jack O'Connell, owns it," said the boy.

"Your dad's Mr O'Connell?" asked Lexey.

"Yes, I'm Finn O'Connell," replied the boy.

"You're Finn?" asked Lexey, astonished.

"Yes, and you're Lexey. Don't you remember, we used to play together as children?"

"I remember playing with you every summer, but then your family stopped coming, and I thought the cottage must had been sold," said Lexey.

"Mum died five years ago," said Finn sadly. "Dad couldn't face coming here for holidays where we'd all been so happy, but we were flooded out at home and he decided this was the safest place to be."

"I'm so sorry about your mum, Finn, that must have been awful."

"It was. I thought nothing could ever be as bad as that again, but now Dad's missing and I've been shot," sad Finn, glaring at Lexey.

"Your dad's missing?" replied Lexey, realising she just kept parroting his statements like an idiot, but her brain felt like it was in overload.

"Yes. We got here about two weeks ago, and then a few days later, Dad drove to Thirsk to stock up with supplies. Zak didn't want to go shopping, so Dad left me to look after him, but Dad never returned."

"Was that about ten or twelve days ago?" asked Lexey. "I've lost track of time a bit, but that was about the time Auntie Jenny went missing."

"Yeah, that sounds about right. Wait, your aunt's missing too?" he replied.

"Yes, she went into York to get my mum I thought, probably the same time your dad went to Thirsk, and I haven't heard from either of them again," replied Lexey.

They stared at each other, sharing the realisation that something terrible must have happened to keep their families away from them both. They shared a look of empathy, silently acknowledging how scared each must have felt. As she looked at him, Lexey realised that she could see the old Finn in him, especially in the mop of untidy hair, but he now looked older than his years, his cheeks sunken and his shoulders slumped.

"Why were you in my henhouse, Finn?" she asked, already suspecting the answer.

"I was borrowing some eggs," he replied. "We've run out of food, and I had to get something for Zak at least — he was crying with hunger."

"Oh, Finn, I'm so sorry, you were welcome to eggs, as many as you wanted. It's just the fox killed half the hens and then some creeps have been hanging round, and I was just trying to keep everything safe," said Lexey, tears running down her face. "I didn't mean to shoot you — my finger slipped," she wailed, covering her face in shame.

"If you can fetch Zak, and give us something to eat, I'll forgive you," replied Finn, peeling her hands from her face, and giving her a thin smile.

"Of course," said Lexey, leaping up, "that's the least I can do!"

Having made sure Finn was comfortable, his leg supported on a cushioned stool, a big chunk of cake and a glass of her aunt's homemade apple juice at his elbow, Lexey set off into the night. The blackness was total, with no moon or starlight making it through the thick cloud cover, and no artificial lights anywhere. The bike's weak headlight barely penetrated the darkness, and Lexey could feel panic building up inside her as each push of the peddles propelled the bike blindly into the dark. A few times she hit the grass verge, wobbled, but stayed on, but she still managed to hit every puddle on the way, icy water and mud drenching her repeatedly.

Although it was five years since she had last been there, Lexey found Heather Cottage straight away, despite the complete darkness, having been there so many times as a young girl. There was only one tiny wavering light visible through the cottage window, and Lexey's heart sank as this was obviously a candle. She had hoped there was electricity and a working phone at the cottage so she could call an ambulance for Finn, but the power outage was apparently fairly widespread.

Lexey hammered on the door and the flickering light moved towards the door which was then opened by a boy of about ten. He stared at Lexey in shock, screamed and dropped the candle, plunging them both into darkness. Lexey could hear him running up the stairs and then a door banging, but he'd left the front door open, so after a moment's hesitation she entered the cottage. She felt in her pocket for the torch she'd brought with her, and shone it around, biting back a scream when she caught sight of herself in the hall mirror. No wonder she'd terrified Zak; her hair was a wet tangled mess, her face and clothes sprayed in mud and, worse still, her tee-shirt was splattered with blood.

"Zak," she called out, as she went upstairs, "I'm sorry I frightened you. It's Lexey. Do you remember I used to play with your brother when you were tiny? Well, Finn's at my aunt's farm, and he's, eh, hurt his leg, so asked me to come and fetch you."

Lexey heard a snuffling from behind a door and waited outside, not wanting to force her way in and frighten him further.

"Zak, I know I look scary, and I'm sorry, it's just mud, and well, a bit of your brother's blood, but it really *is* me and I'm harmless," said Lexey quietly.

She felt a bit guilty at the last bit, as she *had* shot his brother, but thought it best not to mention that. There was still no movement from inside the room, and she felt in her pocket for the piece of cake she'd brought with her. It was a bit squashed, but still recognisable as cake, and smelt good, so it might just be enough to tempt a hungry boy out of his room.

"Zak, I have some cake for you here. I'm putting it outside your door and going downstairs, so feel free to take it. If you then want me to take you to your brother, and more cake, I'll be downstairs."

Lexey retrieved the fallen candle and having found some matches in the kitchen, relit it and placed it on the hall table to give Zak some light to come downstairs. She tried the landline phone, but it was dead as she expected. Taking her torch into the kitchen, she dampened a cloth and attempted to clean up her appearance a little, before searching through the kitchen cupboards for anything useful to take back to the farm.

The only food in the cupboards was some dried pasta and the end of a packet of cornflakes. As she picked up the box, Zak, who must have tiptoed down the stairs, ran at her and grabbed it off her.

"That's mine," he said, clutching the cornflakes to his chest and glaring at her.

"It's okay, Zak, I'm not going to take it. I have lots of food at the farm, so if you're hungry. I can soon make you and Finn a lovely meal once we get back there," said Lexey, leaning down to his eye level.

Zak glared at her for a moment longer, and then his face crumpled, and tears ran down it.

"Please," he said, leaning into her, all fight gone out of him.

Lexey hugged him close a moment and was shocked at how thin he was.

"Okay, Zak, let's pack up your favourite toys and a few clothes and then we'll get back to Finn, shall we?"

Zak nodded, wordlessly, and then held tight to Lexey's hand as they went upstairs to find his teddy bear, a couple of books, a few bits of clothes and his and

Finn's toothbrushes. Lexey piled these into Zak's Superman rucksack and then they went to find his bike, which thankfully had a better headlight than hers. Leaving a note in case his dad returned, Lexey locked the door and they set off together across the dark moors.

Chapter Seven

Zak dashed into the farmhouse, and then stopped abruptly when he saw his brother slumped in a chair, his eyes closed and blood seeping through the bandage on his leg. "He's dead," Zak screamed. "Finn's dead!"

Zak started to cry hysterically, and Finn's eyes flew open.

"It's okay, buddy, I'm here, Zak. It's okay," said Finn, sitting up and opening his arms wide.

Zak ran to his brother and clung onto him tightly. Finn grimaced when Zak knocked his leg, but said nothing, just held him close and stroked his back. Not wanting to intrude, Lexey made herself busy cooking them both goats' cheese omelettes, which she served up with chunks of home-made bread. She had long since run out of butter, and had spread cooking margarine on the bread, but the boys didn't care, just devoured the meal wordlessly. To finish, Lexey served them both mugs of cocoa, using her precious only tin of cocoa she was saving for cake making. In the circumstances she thought it was worth it, and seeing Zak's grin, she knew she'd been right.

Leaving the boys to savour their chocolate drinks, Lexey went up to make beds up for them both.

Fortunately, the rambling old farmhouse had six bedrooms, so they could have a room each, but Lexey made sure the boys were next to each other in case either woke in the night and needed the comfort of their brother. Lexey hesitated before raiding her late uncle's wardrobe, and then realised she was being silly — he didn't need them any more and Finn did. She laid pyjama bottoms, a couple of tee-shirts and some shorts out on his bed; they would probably be too big for him but would be better than nothing.

Zak was almost asleep already, so she showed him to his room and then helped Finn upstairs. Although Lexey was exhausted, there was one thing she needed to do before going to bed, so picking up the torch, she went back out into the black night. She retrieved the shotgun from the yard and removed the second round, before locking the gun and the ammunition back in the gun cabinet.

After checking the doors were locked, Lexey went up to her own bedroom, and her eyes immediately fell on the other shotgun propped up in the corner. She never wanted to risk shooting someone by mistake again, and with a child in the house, didn't want to risk him playing with it and it going off accidentally. Too tired to go back downstairs with it, she removed the rounds and dropped them into her bedside drawer before shoving the gun under her bed out of sight.

She could hear Zak and Finn moving around, and it seemed strange to have someone else in the house, but somehow comforting; for the first time in over two weeks, she was not alone.

A noise woke Lexey from a nightmare, her heart beating out of her chest. It took her a few moments to realise that it was just one of the boys going to the bathroom and not an intruder. Once they had returned to their room, she tried to go back to sleep but the nightmare stayed with her, and she couldn't settle. In her dream she'd fired a gun at a noise and then shone her torch to see her mother laid on the ground with a hole in her chest.

She knew that hadn't happened, but the image stayed with her, seared onto the inside of her eyelids. She missed her mum so much and couldn't shake the feeling that something was very wrong.

"Look after yourself, Mum, and come back to me soon. I love you," she whispered into the night.

It was nearly dawn before Lexey eventually fell into a troubled sleep, and mid-morning before she awoke. She staggered downstairs to find Zak and Finn had fed the chickens and goats and made a pan of porridge.

"We didn't know if we should stay or go, whether we should wake you up or leave you to sleep," said Finn.

"And we didn't know if it was okay to help ourselves to breakfast," said Zak, "even if it was just yucky porridge."

"Of course it was, Zak," said Lexey, with a grin, "and if you want to go and collect some eggs, you can have a brunch of scrambled eggs on toast to make up for the yucky porridge."

"Yeah!" said Zak, picking up a basket and dashing outside.

"Slow down," Finn shouted after him. "Be very careful picking up the eggs — we don't want to break any."

"I will," came back the shouted reply.

"I doubt it," said Finn to Lexey with a grin. "That kid's never been careful in his life."

Lexey, busy making a cup of tea, turned and grinned back at Finn over her shoulder, and then started to laugh.

"What?" asked Finn realising she was laughing at him.

"Nothing," replied Lexey, turning back to the range and smothering her laugh. However, as soon as she took her bowl to the table and caught sight of Finn she started to laugh again.

"Sorry, Finn," she said, "it's just you look so funny in my uncle's clothes!"

The shorts came down to his calves and flared around him like a skirt and the tee-shirt hung off one shoulder and was nearly as long as the shorts. He probably could have got both legs in one side of the shorts, and she could have worn the tee-shirt as a dress.

"I thought I looked very elegant," said Finn pretending to be indignant.

Finn stood up and attempted to do a twirl, but quickly sat down again with a look of pain on his face.

"Here, let me look at that," said Lexey, all humour forgotten.

She abandoned her tea making, knelt down and gently removed the soiled dressing from his leg. The bleeding had stopped but the skin around the gouge was red and inflamed. Lexey fetched the antiseptic and bathed the leg again before applying a clean dressing.

"Thank you," said Finn, putting his hand on her shoulder.

"No need to thank me," said Lexey, "it's the least I could do, seeing as it's my fault you're hurt."

She looked up and found herself looking into his startlingly bright blue eyes, unable to look away. She may have remained on her knees staring into Finn's eyes all day if Zak hadn't burst back through the door with his haul of eggs.

"I've got loads!" he cried, thumping the basket on the table in front of them.

Almost in slow motion, an egg rolled out, and Lexey, still in a daze, just put her hand out without thinking and caught it as it fell towards the floor.

"Gosh, that was lucky," said Zak.

"I'm in the cricket team at school," said Lexey, standing up and putting the egg back into the basket, "so I'm used to catching balls, or eggs in this case."

She grinned at Zak, and, keen to put some distance between herself and Finn until she'd analysed what had just happened, took the basket to the range and got out the frying pan.

"Okay, scrambled eggs coming up," she said.

"Great," said Zak, jumping up and down. "Finn, can we stay here please?"

"That's not up to me, Zak," said Finn, "but if Lexey will let us, I'd like that too."

"Can we, Lexey, can we?" asked the excitable Zak.

"Well, I'd like it too," replied Lexey, turning from the stove and looking over Zak's head at Finn. "I'd like that very much."

"Were you lonely on your own, Lexey?" asked Zak.

"Yes, I was," said Lexey. "Lonely and a bit scared too"

"I was scared too when Finn left me to come here," said Zak, "and even more scared when you arrived looking like a ghoul."

They all laughed, and the atmosphere lightened. Before long they were all tucking into scrambled eggs, and Lexey put the strange moment earlier to the back of her mind for now.

Chapter Eight

As it was raining heavily again, they stayed inside all day, Zak drawing on a pad Lexey had found for him, and Finn reading one of Aunt Jenny's detective novels. Lexey started to make some bread, leaving the dough to rise whilst she made a chocolate cake as a treat for them all. Zak left off his drawing to 'help' her and was happily licking out the bowl whilst she put the cake in the oven.

It was a lovely domestic scene, Finn sitting by the range, Zak with chocolate smears across his face drawing contentedly, and the smell of baking chocolate cake filling the room. Lexey found herself singing quietly as she kneaded the bread and realised that for the first time in a long while she was happy.

This pattern of simple domesticity continued as the week progressed, looking after the animals, cooking and eating together, playing old board games of Aunt Jenny's, reading in quiet companionship. Apart from regularly redressing Finn's leg, to Lexey, it felt like all the family holidays she had had at the farm over the years, and she could almost believe that her mum, dad and Aunt Jenny had just popped out and would be back soon.

Lexey was brought back to reality when she used the last of the porridge oats one morning. Whilst searching the pantry for more, she realised they were running low on all basic supplies. Whilst there were loads of jars of her aunt's preserves, she only had the end of a packet of flour, a couple of blocks of margarine, three packets of pasta and one of rice. There were about ten tins of tomatoes, six of baked beans, and apart from jars of herbs and spices, that was about it.

Lexey stared at it in horror. With three of them, one an ever-hungry child, they had got through almost everything in the pantry in a week. How on earth were they going to survive if help didn't come? Not wanting to worry Zak, she waited until he had gone out to collect the eggs, his favourite chore, before sitting down with Finn to discuss the problem.

"I'm so sorry, Lexey," said Finn, "if you hadn't taken us in, you'd be okay for food."

"I'd have run out eventually," replied Lexey, taking his hand briefly, "and you'd have both been dead!"

Finn squeezed her hand, and Lexey felt his strength flow into her.

"We'll find a way, Lexey," he said, and she felt some hope return.

It had stopped raining, and a watery sunshine made everything look more cheerful as they walked around the farm taking stock of what they had. Aunt Jenny's vegetables were coming on nicely but not many of them looked ready to harvest. The fruit trees had a good crop growing, some varieties doing better than others, however, it would be the autumn before they were ripe. The remaining chickens were fine, and laying well, and the pigs were fat and healthy, but very soon there would be no food for them either.

Finn and Lexey leant on the rail of the pig pen and watched the pigs snuffling about.

"I don't think I could slaughter one, Finn," said Lexey.

"Not sure I could either," replied Finn. "We used to get our bacon from Braithwaite's farm not far from the holiday cottage. I think they used to butcher their own. If they are still there, maybe we could do a deal with them to butcher ours if they kept some of it?"

"I don't think I could eat them," said Lexey, pulling a face. "It would be like eating friends."

"I know what you mean," said Finn. "I'm not sure I could either. Besides, we all eat more or less vegetarian now, don't we? I can't remember the last time I had any meat."

"Me neither," replied Lexey. "Once everyone realised that meat farming was another factor in CO_2 emissions, it just became taboo, didn't it?"

"Yeah," said Finn, "but just sometimes I really fancy a bacon sandwich."

One of the pigs grunted loudly, almost in protest.

"No, not you, Freddy, I couldn't eat you," said Finn, reaching in and scratching the pig behind its ears.

"Freddy!" exclaimed Lexey. "You named them?"

"Of course," replied Finn with a grin. "That's Cyril, that's Susie Sue, that's Zak…"

"You named one after your brother?" asked Lexey, incredulously.

"Well, he looks like him, and Zak eats like a pig. In fact, they could be brothers," replied Finn.

"Well, that would mean, piggy Zak was *your* brother too!" said Lexey, with a laugh.

"Hm, never thought of that," said Finn, "and I absolutely couldn't eat a family member."

"How about we see if the Braithwaites will take the pigs off us, in exchange for something else?" suggested Lexey. "Flour, butter, oats, hens, candles — anything really — as we can't feed the pigs much longer and I couldn't stand by and watch them starve."

"Good idea," replied Finn. "Why don't I cycle over to see them this afternoon? If I can borrow your bike, I'll go by the cottage afterwards, get mine, and wheel them both back. I seem to remember a kid's bike trailer Dad used for Zak when he was small, and if I can find that I'll be able to bring back some clothes and anything else useful."

"Great idea," said Lexey. "Why don't you take Zak, and then you can take turns to wheel the spare bike?"

"Good plan," agreed Finn. "Will you be okay on your own?"

"Hah," Lexey replied, hands on hips, "I survived for weeks before you turned up, mister!"

"What are you two talking about?" said Zak, running up to join them by the pigpen.

Lexey and Finn looked at Zak, looked at piggy Zak and burst out laughing.

"What?" said Zak, indignantly.

"Nothing, buddy," replied Finn, trying not to catch Lexey's eye. "How about you and I go for a little bike ride?

"Yeah!" replied Zak, and before long the two brothers were pushing off out of the farmyard.

"Bring back any toothpaste and soap from the cottage," Lexey shouted after them.

"Will do," Finn shouted back, waving over his shoulder as they disappeared over the hill.

Lexey stood for a while, looking at the empty road. In truth she had become so used to them being around, she immediately felt a bit lost without them. Giving herself a shake, she decided to make the best of the good weather and weed the vegetable patch behind the house. The sun was warm on her back, and she hummed to herself as she worked, enjoying the fresh air and the physical exercise after so long inside. She was delighted to find rhubarb, spinach, spring onions and globe artichokes that were ready to harvest. She wasn't sure how to cook them all, but fresh fruit and veg was just what they needed.

Lexey stopped for a moment to stretch her aching back and listen to the birds sing. One song soared above the other, and she looked around her and searched for the bird. She soon spotted a blackbird, high up in a tree, singing its heart out, the pure notes rising and falling in waves of natural joy. As she listened, she became aware of another sound, an unnatural sound growing louder by the second. A vehicle was driving up to the farm.

Standing between the trees shading the vegetable patch, Lexey watched as the vehicle came into sight. It was the black pick-up, and with a gasp, she stepped back well out of sight. The vehicle pulled up in the yard, and ponytailed Shaun and the driver with the unkempt beard got out, skulked around the yard, and then banged on the door.

"No one here," said the driver, after a few moments. "Told you she wouldn't survive!"

"Pity," said Shaun, "she was a bit of all right."

"Yeah, well I'm more interested in what they left behind," replied the driver, trying the door handle.

"Hey, it's open! We're in luck!"

Chapter Nine

The two men snuck inside, and as Lexey watched from behind the trees, they started to come in and out carrying her aunt's possessions. The old DAB radio, a bottle of whisky and then all the tinned food piled into a box. Lexey was incensed, they hadn't much left anyway, and these thugs were taking what little they had. She was not going to let them get away with it.

Lexey waited until they went back inside and then crept up to the truck and removed the keys. Tucking them into the pocket of her jeans, she crept round the building and quietly opened the front door. She could hear the men were still in the kitchen, whooping when they found a basket of eggs.

"We should take the hens then we can have eggs every day," she heard one of them say.

"Over my dead body," mumbled Lexey to herself.

She crept up the back stairs, intent on saving the jewellery that her aunt had left behind on her dressing table. Picking up the heavy wooden jewellery box, she tiptoed into her own bedroom, intending to hide it amongst the books on her bookcase. As she moved books aside to make a space behind them, one fell onto the floor with a bang and Lexey froze. She held her breath and listened, but Shaun must have tiptoed upstairs, because suddenly he slid silently into the room.

"What have we got here?" he said quietly.

Without taking his eyes off Lexey, he closed the door behind him and turned the key in the lock. He held his hand out for the box, and Lexey put it behind her back, backing away from him until the back of her legs met the bed.

"Get out of my house," shouted Lexey.

"Your house? I thought this belonged to some old biddy. Dead now, probably," he replied, with a cruel laugh.

"My aunt is very much alive," retorted Lexey, her lip trembling at the thought of her being dead.

"Oh yeah? Doesn't matter, she's not here now. It's just you and me," he said with a leer.

His hand shot out and he grabbed her arm, his nails digging into the flesh. Whether by design or accident, his finger caught a nerve in her arm, and an agonising pain shot down her arm and into her neck. Lexey tried not to scream, but a sob escaped her, and Shaun grinned.

"Now, give me the box," he demanded.

Lexey shook her head, and he squeezed tighter, and whilst she fought the pain, he simply took the box from her hand. He pushed her hard and she fell onto the bed behind her. Before she could move, he was on top of her, pinning her down with a knee on each thigh. At least he'd let go of her arm, which throbbed as blood returned to it, but the pain in her legs grew as his full weight pressed on them.

Shaun opened the box and tipped the few pieces of jewellery onto his hand, her aunt's engagement ring, her late uncle's wedding ring, the pearl necklace given to mark a special wedding anniversary. None were particularly valuable, but all were priceless.

"What a load of rubbish," said Shaun dismissively, dropping the box on the bed and shoving the jewellery into his pocket.

"Still, you can be the consolation prize!" he said with a grin.

Lexey tried to wriggle away, grasping the quilt to try and get some purchase, but getting nowhere. Her legs were going numb, and panic was setting in when her hand brushed against the jewellery box and her fingers closed around it. As Shaun lowered his face towards hers, she swept her hand up and smashed the box against the side of his head with all her might. The box shattered, and Shaun fell to one side, beads of blood appearing amongst the embedded splinters on his temple.

As his weight came off one leg, Lexey quickly pulled her knee up and kneed him hard in the side. Shaun toppled over onto the bed and she rolled away from him, falling off the bed and landing heavily on the floor.

"Don't think you can get away from me," Shaun growled, staggering to his feet.

But Lexey was on her feet too, and in her hand, the shotgun she'd grabbed from under the bed. Feet firmly planted, hand steady, she pointed the gun straight at Shaun's face.

"Whoa," said Shaun, hand raised in surrender. "No need to get nasty, we were just having a bit of fun."

"Fun," spat out Lexey, "fun! You think attacking a defenceless girl and stealing the food from others is fun!"

"We were hungry," whined Shaun, edging towards the door.

"And you didn't care that we would be hungry if you stole our food?" retorted Lexey.

Shaun just shrugged, and Lexey felt her anger grow.

"And the jewellery, the radio, my aunt's stuff! What's your excuse for helping yourself to that?"

"Dunno," mumbled Shaun. "Thought maybe we could trade it for food?"

He pulled the pieces of jewellery from his pocket and threw them on the bed. Lexey glanced at them for a split second and Shaun took the opportunity to launch himself at her. She sidestepped neatly and his head crashed against the window frame. Before he had time to recover himself, the gun was inches from his face, and he was looking down the barrel at Lexey's narrowed eyes.

"Out," she commanded, indicating the door with her head. "Slowly and quietly. I won't hesitate to shoot if you run or alert your partner."

Shaun turned the key in the door and set off down the steps, Lexey right behind him, the gun pointing at his head remaining level and steady all the way,

The other man was still in the kitchen, munching his way through the last of the bread, but nearly choked when he saw Shaun appear, his hands in the air and the gun pointed at his head. Not pausing to save his mate, he turned and ran for the truck, climbed inside and fumbled for the keys.

"You'll get the keys once you've unloaded everything you've stolen," said Lexey, as she and Shaun emerged from the doorway. "Help him, Shaun," she commanded.

The two men hurriedly took everything off the truck bed and piled it in the yard in front of Lexey. She remained static, the gun trained on them the whole time.

"Now, get in the truck," she ordered once there was nothing left to unload.

Once they were inside, she fished the keys from her pocket and threw them through the open window, never once letting the gun drop, even when she was holding it one handed.

"If I see either of you ever again, I'll shoot you on sight, so if you know what's good for you, you'll get as far away as possible," she said quietly.

The two men needed no encouragement to start the engine and reverse out of the yard at speed before disappearing down the farm road in a cloud of dust.

Chapter Ten

Lexey remained in the yard, gun still raised, and watched the dust cloud get smaller and smaller, moving in the direction of the lake. Once she couldn't see it any more, she lowered the gun and slumped against the door frame, and it was there that Finn and Zak found her on their return shortly afterwards.

Finn froze when her saw the gun and pushing Zak behind him, raised his arms.

"Don't shoot, Lexey," he implored.

Lexey glanced down at the gun still clasped in her hands and gave a shaky laugh.

"It's not even loaded," she said, dropping it on the ground and running towards them.

Finn put his arms around her and held her tight as she started to shake and cry. Zak slipped in between them, and the three of them stood together for a long time. When she was calm again, they took her inside and made her a cup of tea, using fresh cow's milk brought from the Braithwaites' farm. Whilst Lexey sat there at the kitchen table, savouring the tea and the relief of having survived, Finn and Zak brought the pile of food and other items inside and put them away.

When they'd finished, Finn sat with Lexey quietly, holding her hand whilst she told him what had taken place. He found himself getting increasingly angry at the thought of what might have happened if she hadn't been so calm and brave.

"The Braithwaites warned us about a couple of farmhands they had sacked a week or so ago for laziness and theft," said Finn. "I think it must have been them, as the Braithwaites thought they might still be around because food and other stuff has been going missing from farm buildings. We are going to need to be really careful because if they're hungry, they will be desperate and dangerous."

"Actually, I think they might have gone," said Lexey. "They drove towards the lake and didn't return. That was why I was waiting outside, I was waiting to ensure they didn't come back and sneak onto the farm. I think the lake must have dried up enough to cross, otherwise they'd have had to come back this way."

"You may be right," agreed Finn. "Tomorrow we'll walk to the viewpoint and have a look, but in the meantime, we need to be really careful."

"I think we need to be careful anyway," said Lexey, thoughtfully. We are lucky and have most of what we need here, but there will be those that have lost everything in the flooding and don't have food or somewhere dry to stay."

"Life as we know it is changing," agreed Finn, "and those that have will have to defend it from those that haven't."

"What a pity we can't just all help each other," said Lexey, sadly.

"Well, I hope most people will, and certainly the Braithwaites will be a big help to us," said Finn. "They have sent us some milk, flour and oats as a present."

"That's great!" exclaimed Lexey, cheering up a little. "Seeing as those pigs ate the last of the bread; now we have extra flour, I can make some more."

"Well, it's even better than that," said Finn, picking up a jam jar full of bubbly beige goo. "They've sent a jar of living yeast, and if you keep feeding it with flour and water every day, it will keep doubling in size and you'll always have yeast to bake with!"

"Wow," said Lexey, taking off the lid and sniffing it, "that's amazing! I had very little dried yeast left, and fresh is so much better anyway."

Whilst Lexey set about mixing and kneading dough, Finn and Zak told her all about the Braithwaites' farm. They had lost all their pigs to swine 'flu a year or so before, and now that people were eating less meat anyway, they had moved into arable farming instead. However, they did miss their pigs, and wanted just a few for themselves, so would love to have Aunt Jenny's pigs.

"It's them who are renting the arable land from your aunt," said Finn. "They had been experimenting with varieties of wheat and oats that grow well in wetter conditions.

"They have even been growing rice in the fields that are flooded most of the time," said Zak excitedly. "We watched a programme on growing rice in China at school, and I never knew we could do it here."

"They also have some pretty impressive wind turbines set up, and even have a little wind powered mill set up to make their own flour and rolled oats. They are self-sufficient for electricity and water pumping, so were unaware of the ongoing power outage," said Finn.

"That's what we need," said Lexey, glumly. "We'll run out of candles fairly soon, and then I don't know what we'll do."

"Well, the Braithwaites have a working landline, so they said they would contact the electricity company for us, but in the meantime, if there *is* a way through to Helmsley now, we could hopefully buy some more candles," suggested Finn.

"We'd have to see if we can sell some eggs or something to pay for candles and anything else we need," said Lexey. "I don't have any actual money, have you?"

"I'd not thought of that," replied Finn, "a few pounds only. Normally I'd pay with my phone, but that's dead, and even if I could charge it, I'm not sure if I have any money. Dad used to deal with all that."

He was quiet for a moment, thinking of his father, and Lexey, reading his mind, gave him a hug.

"Any sign of him at the cottage?" she asked.

"No, it was just as you'd left it, the note still on the table," Finn said sadly. "I found the bike trailer and attached it to my bike. It's outside, full of our clothes and whatever toiletries I could find. Come on, Zak," he said, turning to his brother. "We'd better get it unloaded and stored away out of sight; I think we need to be more careful of security now."

Lexey knew he was right, and whist Zak and Finn were unloading the trailer, after collecting the fruit and vegetables she had harvested, she picked up the shotgun, before fetching another one from the gun cabinet. Whilst Zak was putting his clothes and toys in his room, she and Finn discussed the weapons and agreed they would keep one gun in the hall broom cupboard, and the other under Lexey's bed as before. Both would be loaded, and they would talk to Zak about how important it was that he never touched them. They looked at each other nervously, neither happy about the decision, and feeling the weight of responsibility heavy on their young shoulders.

Whilst the dough rose for a second time, Lexey made a goats' cheese and spinach tart, and for pudding, a rhubarb and apple crumble, adding apple slices from her aunt's preserves to the rhubarb she'd picked earlier. They all ate hungrily, enjoying the welcome change of diet.

Whilst they ate, Zak chattered excitedly about the Braithwaites' farm and their granddaughter, Amy, who he had played with there. Finn teased him about having a girlfriend, and although Zak protested loudly, he also blushed bright red, which made Finn tease him even more.

Once the bread had baked, the washing up had been done, and Finn had checked and double checked that all the doors were locked, they all had an early night, worn out with the events of the day.

Chapter Eleven

The next morning dawned bright and clear, a rare sunny day, and they all felt much more cheerful. The fears of the previous day faded in the sunshine, and after a good breakfast of homemade bread and fresh eggs, Lexey and Finn set off to walk to the viewpoint. Zak had discovered a pile of vintage *Beano* comics in his bedroom, and they couldn't persuade him to leave them for a walk in the sunshine. Lexey wasn't happy leaving him alone, but Finn just shrugged and said they wouldn't be long, but he did make sure that Zak locked the door after they'd left.

As they walked along a road flanked with heather and bracken, steam rose from the wet undergrowth as the sun got hotter. Lexey took off her hoody and tied it around her waist, enjoying the feel of sunshine on her bare arms. Her hair was hot on her neck, and she felt in her jeans' pocket for a scrunchie, and then pulled her hair up into a high ponytail. She felt Finn's eyes on her and smiled at him; her heart skipped a beat when he smiled back, his blue eyes even bluer in the sunshine.

They left the road and picked their way across the moorland tussocks towards the rocky outcrop. Lexey remembered the last time she'd been here; cold, wet, injured and alone. Thinking he'd laugh at it, she told Finn about her being face down in the mud, her ankle caught and twisted, and then having to spend the night in the shooting hide.

"You could have died!" he exclaimed, shocked, "and then I'd never have met you again."

"Well, seeing as I shot you when we did meet, maybe that would have been a good thing," she replied.

"Lexey, a world without you in it would never be a good thing," Finn said seriously, taking her hand.

They looked at each other for a long moment, and then, still holding hands, climbed the rocks and stood looking out across the valley below. Today the colours were bright greens, limes and oranges, with touches of purple where the heather was just starting to flower. There were still puddles of water sparkling in hollows, but the silver lake in the valley was much smaller than when Lexey had last seen it. Finn squinted his eyes and stared at it.

"Look, Lexey," he said, pointing. "I think the line of the road has been marked out with a rope or something, perhaps marking a safe crossing point?"

As they watched, a large red car approached from the other side, and gingerly made its way across the water, keeping between the lines. Waves of water splashed either side, but it got safely through and then started up the hill towards them. They lost it in the twists and turns of the road, but suddenly it was speeding past, and Lexey stared at it, hoping against hope it was her mother returning. She got a fleeting impression it was a man, and sank down on the rock, disappointed.

Finn seemed to read her mind and put his arm around her shoulder.

"I miss Mum," Lexey said, "but if I knew she was safe, I'd be happy, even if I never saw her again."

Finn sighed, thinking of his own mother, and Lexey realised how insensitive her remark was.

"I'm sorry, Finn," she said, squeezing his hand.

"I'd give anything to just see my mum again," Finn said sadly. "When she became ill, I wasn't much older than Zak is now, and I didn't really understand. She tried to hide it from us, and kept cheerful right to the end, but it must have been such an effort for her."

Finn shook his head sadly and remained quiet for a moment, before continuing.

"I just thought she'd get better again soon, and I was more interested in playing football than going to the hospital. I would sulk when Dad insisted that I went with him to visit, especially as Zak, who was only five, was allowed to stay with Grandma."

He shook his head again, and Lexey just waited for him to carry on.

"If I could have my time again, I'd have spent every minute possible cuddled up to her in that hospital bed whilst she read me stories in a scratchy voice."

They sat for a long time looking out over the valley whilst Finn looked back in time and, perhaps for the first time, really mourned his mother. Tears ran down his face, and Lexey gently wiped them away, but said nothing; she was just there for him as he got it all out of his system. Eventually the tears stopped, and, with a new closeness between them, they walked slowly back to the farm, hand in hand.

It was now just past midday and the sun was really hot, but realising they had left Zak alone for far longer than they had intended, they picked up their pace despite the heat. Arriving back at the farm, they were surprised to find the front door unlocked.

"Zak," shouted Finn, but got no reply.

Finn dashed upstairs to look for him, whilst Lexey went to see if he was with the chickens. They both drew a blank, so systematically searched the whole house and farm together, but still found no sign of Zak.

"You stay here, Lexey, in case he comes back," said Finn. "I'll go and search for him on my bike."

A quick hug, and he was gone, leaving Lexey alone.

The hot day became a humid, stuffy evening, and Lexey felt her nerves begin to fray as she paced around outside, waiting, just waiting, unable to do anything until Finn and Zak returned to her. It was amazing how quickly they had become her family, and she couldn't bear the thought of being alone again.

Eventually she went inside, leaving the door wide open in the hope that a bit of breeze would penetrate the stifling heat of the kitchen. Lexey was running the tap to get some cool water when she heard a noise behind her and spun around, a big smile on her face, expecting to see Finn and Zak.

Standing just inside the kitchen door was a large, haggard looking man.

Chapter Twelve

Lexey screamed and the glass fell from her hand, smashing on the tiled floor.

Finn and Zak raced into the kitchen, Zak going straight up to the strange man and leaning against his side.

"Lexey, this is my dad, nothing to be afraid of," said Finn, putting his arm around her shoulder.

"Oh," said Lexey, taking a shuddering breath. She could now see the likeness between him and Finn and felt stupid for screaming.

"Hello, Mr O'Connell," she said, holding out her hand to him. "Sorry about that — you just gave me a bit of a fright!"

"Jack, please," he replied, taking her hand in both of his. "I'm really sorry to have scared you, Lexey. I'm also sorry I worried you both by not leaving a note when Zak and I went to the cottage."

"That's all right, Mr O'Connell — Jack," replied Lexey, a wave of relief washing away her previous anxiety.

Lexey noticed how pale and thin he was and urged him to sit down whilst she made him some tea. Zak, as usual, was hungry, so Lexey made a plate of jam sandwiches using her aunt's wonderful strawberry jam and the rest of yesterday's bread.

Whilst they ate, Jack told them what had happened to him.

"On the day I drove to Thirsk to do the supermarket run, the rain was relentless, and the roads were terrible, just rivers of water, mud and gravel. I skidded and slid but kept going, knowing we needed supplies. As I got lower down, the flooding got more intense, and suddenly the car went sideways off the road and into a raging river, which sweep it along on its side. The car was filling with water, and I tried to release the seatbelt, but my hands were frozen and I couldn't do it for ages. Then, just as it came free, the car hit something hard, perhaps a tree, and I must have banged my head as the next thing I knew was when I woke up in hospital."

Jack paused and took a sip of his tea, and then both Finn and Zak put their arms around him and hugged him tight.

"We thought we'd lost you as well as Mum," said Zak, who was crying freely.

"Never, son," replied Jack. "Whatever it takes, I'll always be there for you. I'm just cross no one in authority came to check on you. As soon as I was able to speak, I asked them to let the police know you were on your own with no food. They promised they would, but maybe they forgot, or the police couldn't get through to you, or there were just so many other priorities you fell off their list?"

He shook his head sadly.

"It didn't matter, Dad," said Zak, wiping his nose with his sleeve. "Lexey has been looking after us. Well, she had to after she shot Finn, didn't she?"

"You shot Finn?" Jack asked Lexey in astonishment.

"It was an accident, Dad, and I'm fine now," said Finn before Lexey could reply.

"I'm really sorry, Jack, I thought he was a fox!" explained Lexey. "Not that he looks like a fox…" she continued, as Jack looked at her accusingly.

Jack looked at her hard a moment longer

"A fox, eh?" he said, raising an eyebrow and Lexey nodded.

"Well, however my boys came to you, I'm grateful you have looked after them both, and if you promise not to shoot Finn again, I'll forgive you," he said, and then started to laugh.

Everyone joined in and then they tucked into their tea and sandwiches, the sweet jam a rare treat. It was starting to get dark, and Lexey lit candles which they took into the sitting room as that was north facing and cooler than the kitchen. Once they were all sitting comfortably, Jack finished telling them what had happened to him.

"I must have been in the water for a couple of days before I was found, but fortunately the water hadn't got any deeper and the car had finished up with the front end well clear of the water. Thankfully, I was unconscious the whole time as I was in a bad way; hyperthermia, concussion, broken ribs and several other small injuries." Jack shook his head, remembering.

"Oh, Dad, that's awful," said Finn. "I always believed you'd come back, and that it must be something serious keeping you away, but it's probably a good thing we didn't know how close we'd been to losing you."

"Well, it's taken a long while to recover, and for the water to go down enough to cross over, but as soon as I was able, I hired a car and came to get you," said Jack. "I don't know how I thought you'd be surviving, but it was such a shock to find the cottage empty, and such a relief to find the note. I came straight here and was reunited with Zak, and had planned that once Finn returned, I would take them both back to the cottage."

"Oh," said Lexey, her face falling. "I'll miss you all, but, well, of course you'll want to be on your own now. I'll pack up some food for you..." Her voice trailed off.

"It's all right, Lexey, if you don't mind me staying too, Zak is insisting we stay here with you," said Jack.

"Yes please," said Lexey, simply, grinning at them all.

"Phew, that's a relief," said Zak. "Your cooking's better than Dad's!"

"Oi, it's not that bad!" said Jack, ruffling Zak's hair.

"Which reminds me," he continued, "I've got some more food in the car. The reason we were missing when you got back was that we popped back to the cottage to get my things, and then we detoured to the Braithwaites' to get more supplies on the way back"

"That's where I caught up with them," said Finn. "I was really worried, when I found all Dad's stuff missing from the cottage and thought it was those thugs again, so I cycled over to the Braithwaites' to see if they knew anything."

Lexey gave him a hug, knowing how worrying that must have been.

"Anyway, once we'd all been reunited, I made an arrangement for the Braithwaites to come over in a few days to pick up the pigs — I hope that's okay?" asked Finn.

"Yes, great. Thanks, Finn," replied Lexey.

Between them they emptied the car of food and the rest of the O'Connells' possessions from the cottage and made up a bed for Jack in one of the remaining unused bedrooms. Just having an adult in the house made Lexey feel more secure, and whilst she still desperately wanted her mum, dad and aunt to return, for the time being she was happy being part of the O'Connell family.

Exhausted with the day's events, they all had an early night and Lexey soon fell into a deep sleep. She was awoken in the early hours of the morning by a bright light and for a second, she thought it was lightning, a storm that would clear the build-up of heat.

The light remained bright, causing her to wake up fully, and she realised it was the overhead light; electricity had been reconnected.

Lexey turned the light out and once her eyes had readjusted, wandered out onto the landing. She could see lights blazing downstairs, but as the other bedrooms had not been in use when the power outage started, they remained in darkness. She could hear Jack snoring loudly, a deep base note, and a lighter snore which was probably Finn, which made her grin. She'd tease him about it tomorrow.

Lexey tiptoed downstairs and switched lights off, leaving just a small lamp on in the kitchen. She put the kettle onto the hob, and whilst it boiled, leant against the windowsill and gazed out into the night A glorious aurora blazed across the heavens, not just the usual green, but vibrant pink morphing into purple. It was magical, and Lexey watched mesmerised, unaware that Finn had come downstairs until she felt his arm around her shoulders. There was something so very familiar about his presence that she knew instantly it was him without looking, and she tilted her head onto his shoulder, and together they watched the lights dance across the sky.

Chapter Thirteen

Before going back to bed, Lexey prepared a large amount of bread dough, and left it to rise next to the range. When she awoke mid-morning and came downstairs, Jack informed her he had knocked it back, shaped it into loaves and rolls and left it to prove again. Lexey was delighted to find that he did enjoy cooking, despite Zak moaning about it, and as the bread baked and she had breakfast, they chatted happily about favourite recipes and past cooking disasters.

Zak and Finn came in from feeding the pigs and chickens, and both grinned happily at the domestic scene of Lexey and Jack nursing mugs of tea and chatting whilst the kitchen filled with the delicious aroma of baking bread. The boys joined them at the big old kitchen table, and when it had cooled enough, they all shared the first loaf, warm and fragrant and dripping with the Braithwaites' rich butter and Aunt Jenny's homemade jam.

Lexey told Jack of their plan to go to Helmsley market to try and sell eggs and bread. As it was shaping up to be another glorious day, and the solar battery of the car would now be fully charged, they decided to go straight away.

Getting into a car and driving away from the farm after so long at the farm felt very strange to Lexey, and her stomach was full of butterflies as they drove down towards civilisation. Reaching the lake, they saw it was even smaller than the day before. By keeping between the marker ropes and driving slowly, it was like crossing a wide ford and they got across safely. They came out the other side and Jack tested his brakes before accelerating onwards, reaching the market town of Helmsley before long.

The town square was chock-full of vehicles, and each had their boots open or tail gates down and make-shift tables set up alongside. It looked like a disorganised car boot sale and spilled out beyond the square onto the surrounding streets, making finding somewhere to park very difficult. The bottom of the town was still partly flooded and there wasn't much traffic passing through, so Jack just lined his car up alongside others and hoped for the best. They opened up the boot, and before long people were stopping to see what they had to offer.

"What do you need?" asked a man who looked like an old farmer.

"What do you mean?" asked Finn.

"Well, what use is money?" the man replied. "There's very few deliveries getting through to the shops and supermarket, so we are just exchanging what we don't need for what we do."

"Wow, that makes sense," said Lexey. "We have fresh eggs, goats' cheese and bread, what do you have?"

"I keep bees, so I've got honey and beeswax candles," replied the man, who introduced himself as Seth Armstrong. "I'd love some of your bread — it smells wonderful!"

Finn swapped a loaf of bread for a jar of honey, and six bread rolls for six beeswax candles. Before long they had swapped all their produce for a range of delicious foods, including homemade pasta, wild garlic pesto and a couple of bottles of local wine. Lexey had acquired some vegetable seeds, free, from a kind old lady who was singlehandedly trying to keep the old varieties going. The only thing they couldn't get was cocoa, but Jack and Finn tried the little supermarket, and whilst the shelves were bare of fresh produce, they were able to buy the entire stock of cocoa (six tins), along with matches, toilet paper, shampoo and toothpaste.

"I still seem to be able to pay for things with my phone," Jack told Finn. "So as long as I can charge it, and goods are still available, we'll be fine."

"I take it we are staying here then?" asked Finn, hopefully, dreading the answer, in case Jack said they would return to their home.

"I think so, yes. I thought about it a lot whilst I was in hospital, and there is nothing to go back to in Leeds really, is there? Without your mum, the house doesn't feel like a home and you both seem happier here where there are only has happy memories. Mum's life insurance has paid out more than enough for me to give up work to look after you both, so I can be anywhere, and I think it's going to be safer and healthier in the countryside if this flooding continues," said Jack.

Finn was delighted and went off to tell Zac and Lexey the good news. Zac was playing catch with some local children in the square, and Lexey was chatting to the beekeeper.

"Mr Armstrong has been telling me about beekeeping," she told Finn excitedly. He's going to let me have some when they next swarm!"

Finn looked at Lexey in astonishment.

"But Lexey, you don't know anything about beekeeping," he said.

"No, but I can learn, and you can build me a beehive."

"Oh, I can, can I?" replied Finn with amusement. "With the internet down, how are we going to find out how?"

"At the library," replied Lexey, pointing to a town hall like building on one side of the square.

"Wow," said Finn, "I didn't know libraries still existed."

"Well, this one does," replied Lexey. "Apparently, it's been kept open by volunteers all these years, and it's now coming into its own."

"Lead on then," said Finn, slinging his arm loosely around her shoulders.

Jack and Zak had joined them, and together they strolled into the old building and were met with rack upon rack of books, and a warm welcome from the two librarians. One took Lexey to find books on beekeeping and also showed her where there were books on vegetable growing. As she pored over them eagerly, Jack and Finn were also engrossed in books about energy generation, and Zak had found a whole shelf of superhero comics and was in schoolboy heaven.

They filled in the forms to join the library and were issued with library cards. They were only allowed to take out one book each as the time frame for returning them was uncertain if flooding was bad again. Lexey got a book on beekeeping, and Finn used his ticket to get a book on vegetable growing, knowing he would benefit from the results. Jack got a technical manual to do with wind turbines, and Zak spent ages dithering between which superhero book to take home, but eventually settled on Spiderman.

They carefully placed the books amongst their other purchases, aware how precious the knowledge they contained was, and drove happily home. It had been a good day.

Chapter Fourteen

After a late lunch of fresh pasta with pesto stirred through and goats' cheese sprinkled on top, Jack went to see the Braithwaites about a secret idea he had. Finn and Lexey went to look at the vegetable patch and plot out where they would plant the seeds she'd been given. The crops that Aunt Jenny had put in were coming on in leaps and bounds due to the few days of sunshine, and they picked and ate a few early raspberries as they strolled around.

"I think we should build some fully raised beds for the plants that are less happy with constant rain. If we put small stones in the bottom the rain should drain through," said Lexey, who'd been reading a bit of the library book on veg growing over dinner.

"Good idea," said Finn, "but where will we get wood or stones to build them?"

"How about here," said Lexey, stepping through a broken-down dry-stone wall to an uncultivated area of land. There was an old shed that had half fallen down and lots of weeds, but the patch was in full sun, and the soil looked good.

"We can use some of the stone from the wall or wood from the shed for the sides of the beds," said

Lexey, "and collect the smaller pieces of stone for drainage material."

Finn nodded and they grinned at each other, pleased with their plan, and then paced out where the beds would go.

They had planned to start the next day, but before they could make a start, Mr and Mrs Braithwaite arrived, Mrs B in an old Land Rover pulling a horsebox, Mr B a few moments later in a tractor pulling a long trailer. On the trailer was, what looked to Lexey, a pile of metal junk, with several long pieces that stuck out off the end of the trailer. Jack seemed delighted to see it, and he and Mr Braithwaite, with Finn and Zak's help, set about unloading it. Lexey helped Mrs Braithwaite unload the Land Rover, which was crammed with bags of flour and oats, fresh vegetables, milk, cheese and butter. Now that the electricity was back on and the fridge working, fresh food could be kept cool, and Lexey was delighted that she could now really vary their diet.

Lexey and Mrs Braithwaite, who told Lexey to call her Marie, had a pot of tea and a slice of Lexey's delicious chocolate cake whilst the boys fussed around with the bits of metal. Once that was done, they went to round up the pigs, ready to load them onto the trailer. Lexey went to open the horse box up ready, and then jumped back in astonishment. Inside was a horse, the spitting image of Beauty whom she had loved when she was younger.

"Oh, I forgot to mention," said Marie, "this is Joy, Beauty's daughter. She is too old now to help around the farm, and, well, Finn thought you might be able to take care of her for me."

Lexey said nothing, just stood there with her mouth open and stared at the horse. Finn came up and looked at Lexey anxiously.

"I'm sorry, Lexey, maybe I should have asked you first," he said. "We have plenty of fields for her to graze in and you can ride her to get around, so I didn't think it would be a problem and, well, I wanted it to be surprise."

Lexey tentatively reached out her hand and stroked Joy's nose. The horse whinnied softly and nuzzled her nose into Lexey's palm, and then put her head over Lexey's shoulder and pulled her close. Lexey threw her arms around Joy's neck and hugged her tight for a long moment, before turning and hugging Finn and then Marie.

"Thank you," she said simply, her eyes shining with tears.

Whilst Lexey got Joy settled in Beauty's old stable, the others loaded the pigs into the horsebox, and they were gone before Lexey could regret their loss.

It was much later in the day, after a massive lunch using some of their new supplies, that Lexey remembered the bits of junk Jack had been so excited about and asked what it was.

"It's the Braithwaites' original small wind turbine that came down in a storm years ago," he replied. "I'm hoping I can get it up and working again, and then we'll have electricity if there is another power cut."

"Wow, that's brilliant!" Lexey exclaimed. "Do you think you can fix it?"

"Well, the book I got from the library is very helpful, but I'm not sure all the parts of the gear box are there, and one of the drive shafts is cracked and needs replacing, so it may be a long job."

"Uncle Andrew was brilliant at make do and mend," said Lexey with a fond smile of remembrance. "He was a bit of an inventor and always tinkering with stuff, making it work better or repurposing things for another use. If you look in his workshop behind the barn, you might find something useful."

"Can I come?" asked Zak, and together he and Jack went to find the Aladdin's cave of Uncle Andrew's old workshop.

Lexey went out to spend some time with Joy, and when she came back, she found Finn at the kitchen table cleaning a pile of old tack.

"Seeing as I sprung a horse on you, I thought the least I could do is sort out what she needs," he said with a shy grin.

"Thanks, Finn, and thank you again for the surprise. You've made me very happy," said Lexey, kissing him on the cheek.

"Making you happy is all I ever want to do, Lexey," said Finn, looking straight at her with a very serious face.

Lexey blushed and busied herself with rubbing saddle soap into the old leather bridle to hide her feelings. She glanced at him shyly from under her eyelashes, and found he was still looking at her intently. Their eyes met and time seemed to stand still as an unspoken understanding passed between them.

The moment was broken as Zak burst into the kitchen followed a bit slower by Jack.

"Your uncle's workshop is amazing!" exclaimed Zak. "I'm going to be an inventor when I grow up!"

"Well, I don't know about that," said Jack with a grin, "but I did find some bits that might just work."

"Great," said Finn and Lexey in unison, and then grinned at each other.

Whilst Lexey and Finn finished cleaning the tack, Jack and Finn chatted about how best to repair the turbine. Jack checked bits in the reference book and drew rough diagrams, to which Zak added unnecessary twirly bits and other flights of fantasy. The run of dry weather ended with a sudden heavy rain shower, so apart from feeding the remaining animals and checking they were safe for the night, they all spent a pleasant evening together reading and chatting.

The next day was overcast and very humid but dry, so Lexey and Finn made a start on the new vegetable garden whilst Jack tinkered with the turbine's gear box in the workshop. When not running around pretending to be Spiderman, Zak flitted between them, finding and piling up small stones to be used for drainage or 'helping' his dad in the workshop.

By early afternoon, Lexey and Finn had demolished the shed and made good progress in clearing the weeds. They realised they were very hungry and wandered back to the farmhouse to find lunch, expecting to find the ever-hungry Zak waiting for them. It was deserted, so whilst Finn went in search of his family, Lexey threw together a mixed salad to have with a treat of the Braithwaite's cheese.

Finn returned with Jack, but there was no sign of Zak.

"Must have heard it was salad for lunch," said Jack. "He always was a salad dodger!"

Whilst the men washed their hands, Lexey went to the door and called loudly to Zak. She stood in the doorway and listened, knowing she'd hear the squawk of the rooster if he was with the chickens, but all was quiet. A feeling of unrest settled into the pit of her stomach, and still calling out, she went in search of her surrogate little brother.

She found him in the orchard, lying under the biggest apple tree, silent and still, his leg twisted under him at an unnatural angle.

Chapter Fifteen

Jack laid Zak gently along the back seat of the car. He had regained consciousness briefly and mumbled something about being Spiderman, so piecing it together, they thought he must have tried to climb the apple tree and had fallen out. Lexey padded his broken leg with cushions and blankets and strapped both back seatbelts around him the best she could. Jack and Finn got into the front of the car, and they set off for the long journey to the hospital in York, leaving Lexey behind as there was no room for her in the car.

She watched until the car was out of sight, and then turned back into the silent farmhouse. They had only been gone minutes, but already she missed them, having got used to the noise and chaos of her new family. Jack had promised to ring her as soon as he had any news, so Lexey stayed close to the phone, keeping busy doing much needed chores to stop herself brooding.

Taking a basket of washing outside an hour or so later, she was surprised to see that the sky had turned an ominous greeny-purple and that the earlier humidity was now an energy charged oppressiveness. Deciding against hanging the washing on the line, Lexey was just going back inside when a large piece of hail hit her arm, hard. She dashed inside and put down the basket, and, grabbing her aunt's old waterproof, went back out to coax the chickens into their hut. They didn't take much persuading, as the hail was now coming down fast and hard, hitting Lexey painfully on her head and arms as she shooed the chickens to safety.

The hail then turned to torrential rain, so leaving the goats to fend for themselves, Lexey rushed back inside, water running down inside the neck of the coat and her shoes awash. It was now almost as black as night, and as she changed into dry clothes her bedroom lit up repeatedly with lightning whilst the windows rattled with thunder. She wished Finn was here to hold her hand, but having survived thunderstorms on her own before, she stiffened her spine and got herself organised in case the power went out.

Not long afterward, there was an almighty flash of lightning with almost simultaneous thunder, and the lights did go out. Lexey had the old mobile phone in her pocket and switched on the torch function before calmly lighting a candle, choosing one of the beeswax ones so that the kitchen filled with the calming smell of honey. Although she knew it was pointless, she still checked the house phone but there was no dial tone. Knowing Jack couldn't contact her with news of Zak worried her more than the storm raging around the isolated farmhouse.

Eventually, unable to do anything else, and worn out with pacing, Lexey went to bed, leaving a candle burning in the window to guide her friends home.

The sound of a car stopping outside pulled her immediately from her troubled sleep, and she quickly pulled a jumper on over her pyjamas, dashed downstairs and threw open the door.

An unfamiliar couple stood there in the pouring rain, the man supporting a groaning woman who was bent almost double. Lexey, expecting to see Jack and the boys, just stared at them, blinking in the dazzling car headlights. As her eyes adjusted, she realised the women was heavily pregnant, and, from the garbled explanation the frantic man gave her, the baby was more than ready to make an appearance.

Lexey led them into the kitchen and the man lowered the woman onto the old settee in the corner. Lexey lit more candles and stoked up the range before running to fetch towels and sheets. The woman, introduced as Melissa, was now standing, leaning forward and supporting her weight on the table. She was swaying her hips in small circles as the man, Adam, rubbed her back and talked to her calmly. Without taking his eyes off his wife, he told Lexey quietly the baby was nearly here and asked her to make a bed on the floor. Lexey pulled the cushions off the settee, put a layer of towels over them and covered it with a clean sheet.

"I need to push!" cried Melissa.

Adam and Lexey helped her to lay down and Adam knelt between her legs ready to assist, whilst Lexey stood a little uncertainly, not sure if she should intrude. She had watched a video on childbirth in biology at school, but that all seemed a little bit hazy now. Adam looked up at her and gave her a small smile.

"We are going to need something to cut the cords, Lexey, and something to clamp the ends," he said with quiet composure. "Can you see what you can find and put them into a pan of boiling water to sterilise them, please?"

Lexey nodded and dashed off, glad to be given a task to do. She quickly found some sharp scissors but couldn't think what to use as clamps. Looking wildly round the room, she spied the basket of washing that she had not got around to hanging inside and saw the peg bag nestled on the top.

"Will these do?" she asked Adam, showing him two sturdy plastic pegs.

He nodded, barely looking, his full attention on his wife who was crying out in pain.

Hoping that the pegs wouldn't melt, Lexey put the items into a pan and poured hot water from the kettle over them before setting the pan on the range to come to the boil. She knelt beside Melissa and took her hand, not sure what else to do, but instinctively knowing she needed her support.

"I can see the head now, darling," said Adam, "Can you give me a long slow push please?"

Melissa grunted, and, tucking her chin to her chest, pushed with all her might, her face turning red and sweat running down her forehead. She squeezed Lexey's hand painfully, but Lexey didn't let go, just kept muttering words of encouragement whilst she mopped Melissa's brow with her other hand.

"That's it, Mel, the head's out!" cried Adam excitedly. "One more big push and we'll have our baby."

Melissa pushed hard again, and in a whoosh of fluids, the baby slid out into the waiting hands of its father. There was no sound, and the silence was deafening against the background of thunder. Mel struggled to sit up to see, desperately asking over and over again if the baby was all right.

Lexey picked up a towel she had left warming on the range rail and wrapped it around the tiny blood-speckled baby who was rapidly turning blue. She rubbed its frail body hard through the towel, endeavouring to get its circulation going. Adam cleared some mucus from the baby's mouth and then put his mouth over the baby's nose and mouth and blew gently. At first nothing happened, and then baby gasped and then let out an ear shattering wail.

"It's a boy, Mel, a beautiful baby boy," said Adam, his eyes shining with tears.

Leaving them to share the moment, Lexey carefully tipped the boiling water out of the pan and left it to cool a moment before bringing it to Adam. Thankfully, the pegs hadn't melted, and Adam put them on the umbilical cord a couple of inches apart and then cut the cord between them.

Lexey handed him a second warm towel and he wrapped it around the baby before handing him to his mother. The baby instantly stopped wailing and opened his eyes to stare intently at his new world and his adoring parents. For a second, he seemed to focus on Lexey, and she was instantly lost in their blue depths, besotted almost as much as the boy's parents.

Once the placenta had been delivered and disposed of outside by Adam, they helped Melissa upstairs to Lexey's aunt's bedroom and got her comfortable in the big old bed wearing one of Aunt Jenny's nighties. Whilst Melissa breast fed the baby, Lexey tipped her late uncle's pants and socks out of a drawer and then carried the drawer to the bedside. Lined with a thick jumper covered by a sheet, it made a makeshift cot, and the now sleeping baby was laid gently inside.

Lexey then went to the kitchen and made a tray of tea and toast, bringing it back to the bedroom where the three of them devoured it.

"How come you ended up here, Adam?" asked Lexey, wiping toast crumbs from her mouth.

"Well, we set off for the hospital in York in good time as soon as we were sure Mel was in labour," replied Adam. "First babies usually take a long time, so we thought we had plenty of time, but we hadn't planned for the storm. When we got to the valley, what had recently been a ford was a raging river as wide as a lake again, and we couldn't cross."

He paused, remembering the terror of the moment and Melissa squeezed his hand. Lexey's heart sunk, wondering how Finn and his dad and brother would be able to get back to her if the way through was cut off again.

"We turned around and came back over the moors, hoping to get to Scarborough hospital the long way round, but the baby had other ideas," said Melissa, taking up the story. "My waters broke, and I needed to push, but we were in the middle of nowhere with thunder and lightning all around us. Then we saw your light, the candle in the window guiding us to you."

"I've never been more grateful to see a light before," said Adam, "and to see your friendly face at the door."

"We have to thank you from the bottom of our hearts for taking us in and helping deliver our baby," said Melissa. "In fact, we have decided to give him a middle name, named after you so he will always know of your help and kindness."

"Lexey, meet Joel Lex Roberts," said Adam with a grin, indicating the sleeping baby.

"Wow. Thank you," said Lexey. "That's an honour, and it was a privilege to be there at his birth, but I really did very little. You were amazing, Adam, so calm, and you seem to know exactly what to do. Are you a doctor?"

"No," said Adam with a laugh, "but I am a farmer, and I've birthed many sheep and calves in my time. However, I wasn't really very calm inside, it's very different when it's your own son."

"Well, I think you were both brilliant," said Lexey. "I also think you both need to rest, so I'll leave you in peace. You'll find men's pyjamas in the drawers there, Adam. I don't have any nappies, but there are plenty of small towels in the linen cupboard on the landing."

As Lexey made her way downstairs, she wondered why her aunt had never got rid of her late husband's clothes, but she was glad she hadn't, as they were proving very useful.

Too wired to sleep, she set about cleaning the kitchen, returning the cushions to the sofa and putting the soiled towels and sheets into the washing machine. With no power, she couldn't switch it on, but she lowered the old-fashioned clothes airer from the ceiling and hung the washing from earlier on it to dry in the warmth from the range.

When there was nothing left to do, Lexey made herself a drink and stood at the window cradling the cup whilst she watched dawn creep sullenly in. The thunder and lightning had stopped, but the rain was relentless, the yard awash and a river running down the road. The events of the night seemed like a dream, and her thoughts returned to Zak, hoping he was all right, and that very soon they would all be home again.

Wrapped an old wool throw around herself, she curled up on the sofa and drifted into a deep sleep.

Chapter Sixteen

The telephone ringing woke her with a start, her heart hammering in her chest. Despite the dull daylight the room was bright with electric light and Lexey realised that the power must have come back on. She grabbed the phone and was delighted to hear Jack's voice.

"Hi, Lexey," he said, "I'm so glad to finally reach you. I assume the power has been out again?"

"Yes, and I'm so glad to hear you too. How's Zak?"

"He's fine, Lexey. A broken leg as we suspected, but it's been set, and he now has a full-length bright blue cast he is very proud of. He had a bit of concussion, so they kept him in overnight, but he's fine now and about to be discharged."

"Oh, thank goodness!" replied Lexey, feeling a weight lift off her chest. "But I don't think you'll be able to get back today, Jack; I think the valley's flooded again."

"Oh no, I feared as much," said Jack. "Can you go and check it out and I'll ring back in an hour? We want to get back to you as soon as we can — Finn has been fretting about you being all alone."

"Oh, I'm not on my own," said Lexey with a grin, somehow pleased that Finn had been worrying about her.

"Oh?" replied Jack.

"I'll tell you all about it, when you're home," replied Lexey. "I'll ride Joy to the viewpoint, see how bad the flooding is and speak to you again shortly."

After leaving a note for Adam to help himself to breakfast, Lexey pulled on her aunt's coat and a pair of wellingtons and went outside. The rain had finally stopped, and the ground was steaming in the warmth of thin sunshine, creating a hazy glow. Lexey quickly fed the chickens and goats, and then saddled up Joy and rode out onto the silent misty moors. Pheasants ambled haphazardly across the road, breaking into clumsy, panicked flight at the last moment, and a curlew's strident call cut through the silence.

Hitching Joy to one of the tall posts that marked the line of the road for guidance in snow, Lexey rushed to the rocky outcrop and clambered up to look out across the valley. It was difficult to see the full extent of the flooding through the haze, but sunlight glinting dully off water gave her an impression it was indeed a wide lake again. She waited a short while, but no vehicles passed through it to come up the hill, so she assumed it was currently impassable.

The phone was ringing as she dashed back into the farmhouse, and she got there just in time before Jack gave up. They agreed it was foolish to set off, and Jack said he'd find a B and B for a couple of days. The thunderstorms hadn't hit York, so it would be a day or so before rainwater from the hills swelled the three rivers that converged in York and any new flooding occurred. Currently the ancient city was fully open and despite being busy with tourists, there were plenty of places to stay.

"Can you check out my house, please," asked Lexey, "see if everything is okay? If it's dry inside, you could stay there, perhaps?"

Lexey gave the address, explained where a secret key was kept and how to remove the metal shutters, and Jack promised he would go and check it out for her.

"Can you see if there is any information about where my mum and dad are, please?" asked Lexey, her voice forlorn, as thinking about her home made her homesick and miss her own family more.

"Will do," replied Jack. "Gotta go — Zak is trying out his crutches, and I may just need to catch him! Speak soon."

Lexey stood for a moment in the middle of the kitchen, feeling lost, but then the wailing of a new-born baby broke the silence, and she remembered with a grin that she was not alone. She made a tray of tea and carried it upstairs before knocking on the bedroom door. Melissa was propped up in bed with Joel Lex at her breast. She looked exhausted, but radiant, and gave Lexey a big smile.

"Good morning!" said Lexey. "How are you all?"

"Just great, thanks, Lexey," replied Melissa. "Mischief here didn't sleep much last night, so neither did we, but I'm on too much of a high to care."

"Where's Adam?" asked Lexey, looking round the room.

"He's gone back to the farm to feed the animals and bring me back clean clothes and baby things," she said, stroking the baby's soft cap of fair hair. "It's only about five miles away, so we'll be out of your way very soon."

"Oh," said Lexey, disappointed. "You are welcome to stay a few days, if you would like to?"

"Are you sure?" asked Melissa, a look of relief on her face. "Adam will be busy around the farm, and I'm a bit nervous about being alone with the baby. Silly I know, but my mum was going to be here and won't be able to get through now, so it would be nice to have another woman around for moral support."

Lexey glowed at being called a 'woman'. In the last few months, she had coped with far more than most fifteen-year-olds and realised that she did feel she had grown up very quickly.

"I'm sure," she replied. "It would be good to get to know my namesake here, and, well, I could do with the company."

Whilst they drank their tea, Lexey explained to Melissa all about her missing aunt and parents, and how Finn and his family came to be living there. Listening to the story, Melissa realised that Lexey really did need a female friend right now, so she was happy to stay for the good of them both. Joel Lex had finished his feed and fallen asleep in his mum's arms, so they laid him gently in his makeshift cot before Lexey helped Melissa into the shower.

When Adam arrived back, Melissa was sitting at the kitchen table, her hair washed and a serene look on her face. The baby was waving his arms and legs from the depths of a suitably padded washing basket, and Lexey was stirring something on the range.

"Wow, this looks homely!" said Adam.

The ladies grinned at him, and whilst Lexey served up a hearty home-made soup with crusty bread and chunks of cheese, Melissa told him about their plans for her to stay there a few days.

"If you are sure that's okay, Lexey, it would be a weight off my mind. I didn't want to leave Mel alone all day, but obviously I need to look after the farm too."

Over the next few days, they fell into a pattern. Lexey would hear the baby crying in the night, but didn't get up, just turned over and went back to sleep. Once Adam was up and off in the morning, and Joel Lex had had his morning feed, Lexey would take the baby downstairs and keep him amused for as long as she could, so that Melissa could catch up on her sleep. She'd take him back up to Mel when he needed a feed, and then look after him again whilst Mel got herself up and showered. By the time Adam came back, his wife was dressed and downstairs and Lexey had their dinner ready.

The weather had remained dry but hot and humid, and every afternoon, whilst Melissa and Joel Lex dozed on the settee, Lexey would ride Joy to the viewpoint to see how much the water in the valley below had receded. It was difficult to tell, but each day she thought it looked a little less; however, she had yet to see a vehicle come up the hill from that direction.

On day five since Joel Lex's birth, Lexey was sitting on the settee, rocking the fractious baby whilst Melissa had a shower, when she heard a vehicle stop outside. It was almost midday, so she thought it was Adam arriving home a little earlier than usual and didn't get up. The kitchen door was flung wide open, and in rushed Finn. He stopped dead in his tracks and stared at Lexey cradling the baby. His mouth fell open, but no sound came out. Behind him came Zak on his crutches, and he barrelled into the back of his brother, almost losing his balance. Next was Jack, who also stopped in his tracks and stared.

"Come in, guys, and close the door, can't have the baby in a draught," said Lexey, laughing at their faces.

She carefully laid Joel Lex in the laundry basket, and went and hugged first Finn, then Zak and lastly Jack.

"Where did you get the baby?" asked Zak, hobbling over and peering into the basket.

"Whose baby is it, Lexey?" asked Jack, at the same time.

"It's mine," said Melissa, coming into the kitchen.

"Oh, thank goodness!" said Finn, and Lexey stared at him in astonishment.

"What do you mean? You didn't think he was mine, did you?" she asked him, hands on her hips.

"Well, no," said Finn, a bit shamefaced. "I just couldn't work out where he had come from."

Lexey grinned at his discomfort, and then gave him another big hug. Meanwhile, Jack and Melissa shook hands, and Melissa introduced Joel Lex to a fascinated Zak. By the time Adam arrived back for his lunch, a celebration lunch was being prepared, and a chaotic meal ensued. Zak told them about his accident and how brave he had been at the hospital, and Adam told them how amazing Lexey had been helping Melissa give birth. Although Lexey knew Adam was exaggerating her role, she basked in Finn's open admiration.

Once Adam had gone back to the farm, Melissa went for a rest, and Zak and Jack wandered over to the workshop, leaving Lexey and Finn alone in the kitchen with the baby. Lexey rocked him gently in her arms to get him asleep whilst Finn washed up the dinner things. Once Joel Lex was asleep, Lexey went to help Finn, drying up the crockery which was threatening to fall off the draining board.

"You're a natural, Lexey," said Finn, "you really are."

"Thanks, Finn, but it's easy when you don't have to get up in the middle of the night and can hand back the baby when you've had enough."

"Do you want a baby of your own one day, Lexey?" asked Finn, taking his hands out of the sink and turning to face her.

"Yeah, I think so. But not just yet!" she said with a grin. "You?"

"Yes, definitely, at least four, I think."

"Four!" exclaimed Lexey. "Wow, poor woman!"

"Oh," replied Finn, looking crestfallen. "Three maybe?"

"Hum, maybe…"

"Great," replied Finn with a big grin, before turning back to the sink.

Lexey wasn't quite sure what she had just agreed to, but for some reason, suddenly felt ridiculously happy.

Chapter Seventeen

It wasn't until later that afternoon that Lexey remembered to ask Jack whether he'd been to her home in York.

"We did, Lexey. Sorry I should have told you sooner, but with all the excitement of the baby it slipped my mind," said Jack. "We stayed there actually — I hope you didn't mind?"

"Not at all," replied Lexey. "Was everything all right?"

"Yes and no," said Jack. "It took us a bit to get the door open as the wood had swollen, but inside wasn't too bad. A bit of damp in the hallway was really the only evidence of the flood — the shutters did their job well."

"Oh good, that's a relief," said Lexey. "So, what's the bad news?"

"Well, we searched through the pile of post for anything that would give us a clue to the whereabouts of your family, but there was nothing. However, on the kitchen table was a postcard from Spain," said Jack.

"From my dad?" asked Lexey excitedly.

"Yes," said Jack, "but it was posted several weeks ago and must have arrived just before your mum left there."

"What did it say?" asked Lexey,

Jack put his hand in his pocket and pulled out a dogeared postcard with a picture of a Spanish dancer on the front. He handed it to Lexey silently.

'Darling Sarah,' she read. 'I hope this reaches you okay, and you and Lexey are well. I'm afraid I'm not so good — I'm in the Hospital Universitario Madrid with, I think, a bad dose of malaria. I have used all my money to pay for the treatment, and they won't accept credit cards, so I can't book a flight home, but will be with you as soon as I possibly can. Always remember that I love you both, yours forever, Michael xx'

"Oh no, no," cried Lexey. "Poor Dad, poor Mum!"

"Do you think your mum and aunt went to fetch him home?" asked Finn, putting his arm around her shoulders.

"Yes, they must have done. Mum would never have left him there!"

There was nothing anyone could say to console Lexey, and she went to her bedroom to be alone for a while to think about her parents. When she returned to the kitchen an hour or so later, Adam had returned from his farm with news that his mum-in-law would be coming the next day. His little family would therefore return to the farm in the morning, so everyone mucked-in to make a special last supper together. Finn, noting Lexey's pale face and red rimmed eyes, stayed close to her as they worked, his arm around her shoulder whenever he had a free hand.

"Oh, forgot to say, Lexey," said Jack, once they had finished their meal, "I've brought you some more clothes, books and toiletries from your house, and also the pile of post. Most of it appears to be bills which I can deal with for you, but there is one addressed to you."

He rummaged through a pile of letters and passed one to Lexey. She recognised instantly the headed notepaper and her heart sunk — it was from her school. She realised that, in effect, she had been playing truant for the last few months but hadn't even given it a thought. For most of that time, getting to school hadn't been physically possible due to the floods, and having no phone line for ages had also meant she couldn't contact them, but really, she should have rung the school as soon as she could. The letter said the same, threatening to take legal action if she had not returned before her sixteenth birthday, and after that date could evidence that she was in a training scheme or at college.

Lexey's face fell. Her life at school seemed so remote now, and nothing she had learnt had prepared her for the challenges she had faced in the last few months or would face in the future. To go back to school, she would have to return to York, and she knew with utter certainty that her life was now here, on the farm, on the moors — a simple life of self-sufficiency and family, not academia.

Finn was reading the letter over her shoulder and pointed out that the letter was dated three weeks earlier.

"What's the date today?" asked Lexey, who had completely lost track of time over the last weeks.

Finn told her, and Lexey's face broke into a big grin.

"That's all right then. I'll be sixteen in three days' time. I don't have to go back to school!"

Whilst they all digested that it was almost her birthday and they had nothing to give her, Jack's mind turned to more practical matters.

"You still need to be in a programme of training, Lexey, and so does Finn now we have decided that we are staying here. Zak should be in school too — I'd forgotten all about that with the floods and the accident and everything!"

"Nooo!" exclaimed Zak. "I want to stay here. I don't want to go back to my school in Leeds!"

"There's a good school in Helmsley, Jack," said Adam. "Both Mel and I went there, and I'm sure they'd take Zak on if this is now your permanent address."

Zak's bottom lip was still out, so Melissa sought to reassure him, telling him how much fun she'd had at school. It sounded very different to the school Zak had been to, with a 'forest school' and lots of outdoor activities, and Zak soon looked happier.

Meanwhile, Adam had been thinking about Lexey and Finn's dilemma.

"Lexey, do you want to train to be a farmer?" he asked suddenly.

"Yes…" said Lexey, a little uncertainly. "I'd like to learn more about growing vegetables and animal care, but also other stuff like bee keeping and running a farm shop."

Adam nodded. "What about you, Finn?" he asked.

"Well, a bit like Lexey, I'd like to learn to be self-sufficient, but would also like to learn a bit more about the engineering side of farming — the kind of thing Dad's interested in, like setting up a wind generator or keeping a tractor going. Oh, and woodworking – I loved it at school and it would be great to make furniture."

Adam nodded again, and then turned to Jack. "We had an apprentice last year, and the Braithwaites generally take on one or two, as do other farmers and craft persons around the moors. Leave it with me, and I'll see if we can put a package together that the authorities will accept," he said.

"Wow, that would be great," said Jack, "but do you have the time?"

"It's the least I can do after all Lexey has done for us," said Adam with a smile.

That temporarily settled, they all turned their minds to Lexey's upcoming birthday. Each of them was grateful to her for taking them into her home and her heart and wanted to find a way to say thank-you and make her birthday special.

The next morning, they said an emotional goodbye to Adam, Melissa and baby Joel Lex, all of whom had quickly become part of the extended family. The farmhouse seemed quiet without them, but they soon settled back into their day-to-day routines. After seeing to the animals, Lexey and Finn worked on creating the raised vegetable beds, Jack worked on the wind turbine and Zak, hampered by his leg, just got in everyone's way. Fed up with him whingeing, Finn eventually loaded him into the bike trailer and cycled with him to the Braithwaites' farm so that he could play with Amy. They promised to bring him home that evening (along with the present for Lexey that Finn had secretly arranged with them).

Lexey rang her old school and explained she had moved to live at her aunt's (she didn't tell them her aunt wasn't there) and the reasons she hadn't been in touch (exaggerating how long the phone wasn't working). They reluctantly agreed it was pointless her coming back now if she intended to take on a local apprenticeship and said they would pass her details onto North Yorkshire Council who would be in touch in due course to approve any apprenticeship programme.

Jack rang the school in Helmsley and arranged to bring Zak in for a look around the following week; however, it was agreed that as his leg was in a cast, he wouldn't start school till the next term, which Zak was very pleased about.

The morning of Lexey's birthday brought bright sunshine, and Finn, carefully not mentioning her birthday at all, suggested Lexey take Joy out for a ride in the sunshine. Lexey saddled up and set off, a little sad that no one had wished her 'happy birthday' but trying not to mind.

Her spirits rose as she and Joy rode over the moors. The heather was coming into flower, washing the hills in rich purple which was interspersed with the vivid green splashes of ferns. She stopped by a lone tree, bent over against the habitual wind, its trunk a mass of twists and wrinkles like old rope. A skylark rose into the golden air and sang so beautifully it brought tears to her eyes, she felt the world was wishing her 'happy birthday' even if her family and friends had forgotten.

Meanwhile, back at the farm, frantic activity was taking place. Melissa had arrived with the baby and a big birthday cake, the Braithwaites had arrived with Lexey's special present and a basket of food treats, and Zak and Finn were busy putting up homemade decorations. All they needed now was the birthday girl.

Midday came and went, and still there was no sign of Lexey. Eventually, the Braithwaites had to return to their farm, but they said they would have a good look for her on route. Melissa settled Lex into the laundry basket to sleep as if they had never been away, and said she would stay there whilst Finn set off on his bike and Jack and Zak in the car to look for Lexey.

It was Zak who spotted Joy grazing in a patch of sunlit grass just off the road, but when Jack reached her, her reins were trailing on the ground and there was no sign of Lexey. He led the horse back to the car and Zak held the reins through the open car window whilst Jack searched the hillside. Finn then came around the bend and his heart leapt when he saw the horse but sunk again when he found out that Lexey was still missing.

Jack and Finn set off in ever widening half circles, one on either side of the road, using the car as the centre point, and meeting up each time they reached the road again so as not to lose track of each other. They called her name repeatedly, getting no answer, but then Finn imagined he heard a reply and waved frantically to Jack. Neither could see her, but jogged towards the faint sound of her voice, calling as they went, her reply quickly getting more audible. They were almost upon her before they realised where she was, and just stopped themselves in time before they too fell into the old mine shaft that imprisoned her.

Chapter Eighteen

"Lexey, are you all right?" called a frantic Finn, laying on the ground and reaching his hand down towards her. She stretched her hand up towards him, but their hands were a couple of feet apart; she imagined she felt energy flow from his hand to hers across the gap, and immediately felt stronger.

"I'm more or less unhurt, Finn, just bruised and a bit cold," replied Lexey. "I'm very glad to see you — I thought I might be here all night before anyone noticed I was missing!"

Finn felt a knot in his stomach at the realisation that Lexey didn't know how much they loved her, and how scared and alone she must have felt trapped in the dark hole.

"Don't worry, Lexey, we'll soon get you out!" he called, even though he was unsure exactly how they were going to do it.

"I've an idea," said Jack, who'd been peering over Finn's shoulder but turned and ran back to the car.

"How did this happen, Lexey?" asked Finn.

"I don't really know," replied Lexey. "I dismounted Joy to collect some early bilberries and was working from bush to bush, not really looking where I was putting me feet, when the ground just opened up beneath me."

"They used to mine ironstone on the moors, Lexey. I think this must be an old mineshaft that's become overgrown and forgotten."

"Oh yes, I remember coming here on a field trip from school," said Lexey. "We went to Bank Top and studied the remains of the smelting works and then mapped the line of the old Rosedale Valley Railway."

Whilst Finn distracted Lexey by talking about school trips he had been on over the years, Jack returned leading Joy. He removed the multi-tool he always carried in a pouch clipped to his belt and used the tiny knife to cut through the reins at one side close to the horse's head. Jack then dangled the loose end down the pit, but it wasn't long enough to reach Lexey. Taking off his belt, he trimmed the free end of the reins and then threaded it through the belt buckle, making a hole through the reins with a pointed tool so that the buckle pin could grip it securely.

After coaxing Joy to kneel next to the mine shaft and dip her head forward, Jack dangled the leather strip down the hole. It was just long enough for Lexey to grip and wrap around her hand. With Finn and Jack helping hold the weight, they persuaded Joy to stand up and back up slowly, gradually pulling Lexey up the shaft. Although she felt like her arm was being wrenched off, she didn't let go, and as soon as her free hand was out, Finn grabbed it and helped pull her clear.

Lexey lay on the ground, panting and rubbing her hand where the leather had cut in. Finn lay next to her, his arms around her, holding her close. Jack had unbuckled his belt from the reins and done his best to tie the reins back together; they were a little short now but would do to get Joy and Lexey back home. Finn helped Lexey to her feet and assisted her to mount the horse, before leading it back to the road. Lexey insisted she was fine to ride, but they followed her slowly in the car to make sure she was okay.

As she came into the yard, Lexey spied the ragged banner Zak had made, 'Happy Birthday Lexey', and burst out laughing. What a birthday it had turned out to be! Inside the farmhouse, she was greeted by Melissa and Joel Lex, more birthday banners and a birthday cake with sixteen candles on it. Her heart swelled with happiness, she was alive, she had friends who loved her, and it was her birthday.

By the time she had showered off the mud, washed her hair and changed into a pretty dress, Adam had joined them, bringing with him some homemade beer. Marie and Stephen Braithwaite came back again not long afterwards, bringing with them their granddaughter, Amy, much to Zak's delight. The party was lively, and the party games even more so, helped along by the beer, a little of which Lexey was allowed mixed with Marie's homemade lemonade.

They were making so much noise they almost didn't hear the phone ring, and it took Lexey a moment to register what the unfamiliar sound was and pick up the receiver.

"Happy birthday, darling," said the voice in her ear.

"Mum? Mum? Is that you?" cried Lexey.

"Yes, darling, it's me. Hang on a moment, I've someone here who really wants to speak to you too."

"Hello, Lexey. Happy birthday, my darling girl," said her father.

"Dad! Are you all right?" cried Lexey in disbelief.

"I'm getting there, love. Not a hundred percent yet, but considerably better than I was before your mum and aunt rescued me."

"Is Auntie Jenny there too?"

"I am," said Jenny, who'd grabbed the phone from Michael. "Happy birthday, Lexey!"

"Where are you all?" asked Lexey.

"We're in France, but hopefully crossing in the morning," said her mum who had taken back the receiver. "With any luck, we'll be with you in a two, or three, days' time."

"Brilliant!" said Lexey, but before any more could be said, the connection was lost.

Lexey turned to face her now silent friends, tears streaming down her face.

"They're coming home! Mum and Dad and Aunt Jenny are coming home!" she said, before grabbing Finn and whirling him round in joy.

Everyone cheered, and glasses were refilled in a toast.

"To family and friends," said Lexey.

"To family and friends," they all chorused.

A little later, Finn told Lexey to close her eyes and led her outside and to the area they had been making into the new vegetable garden. Lexey giggled all the way, trying to guess what her present was going to be.

"Okay, open your eyes now," said Finn.

Lexey opened her eyes, and looked around, but it took her a moment to realise what her present was. Standing at the bottom of the garden next to the wildflower meadow was a simple white beehive.

"Thank you so much, Finn. It's perfect," cried Lexey, throwing her arms around him.

"Not many sixteen-year-old girls would think a beehive is a perfect present," said Finn, laughing with relief. "But then, you are not a normal sixteen-year-old!"

"I'm not?" teased Lexey. "Is that good or bad?"

"It's good, Lexey. You are perfect. Perfect for me, anyway," said Finn.

And then he kissed her.

Chapter Nineteen

Over the next couple of days, Lexey frantically cleaned and baked, getting the house ready for her aunt and parents' return. Keeping busy also stopped her thinking too much about 'The Kiss'. She had not really been alone with Finn since as the rain had returned with a vengeance and they couldn't work on the new vegetable garden. Finn was helping his dad in the workshop instead. It felt to Lexey a bit like he was avoiding her, but she told herself not to be paranoid.

Lexey had other things to worry about anyway, mainly the continuing rain which could mean that the valley would be too flooded for her family to reach her. She was also worried what her aunt may think about her inviting Jack and his boys to move in with them. They could, of course, move back to their holiday cottage, but Lexey wanted them to stay. To her they felt like extended family, or maybe, in Finn's case, something much more, but then she wasn't letting herself think about that.

After Lexey's fall down the mine shaft, Finn wasn't keen on her riding out on Joy by herself, especially in the drenching rain, so on the morning of day three Jack drove down to the valley to check on the flooding.

Lexey could tell by his face as soon as he returned that the news wasn't good but hoped against hope they would still get through. As the day wore on with no sign of her family, she resigned herself that they were not coming, and consoled herself that as long as they were all safe, it didn't matter if it took a few days longer to get to her.

Later that afternoon, Lexey was arranging a vase of wildflowers in the room she had prepared for her parents when she heard a raised voice downstairs. She went to the bedroom door and just caught the next sentence being shouted in a woman's voice.

"Who the hell are you, and what are you doing in my kitchen!"

Lexey instantly recognised her aunt's voice, and dashed downstairs and into the kitchen.

Her bedraggled aunt was standing with her hands on her hips glowering at Zak who looked terrified. Water was running off her drenched clothes, forming a puddle on the floor around her. Poor Zak was wobbling on his crutches with one hand in the cookie jar whilst trying to back away without letting go of the biscuit. Lexey leapt forward, caught him as he toppled over, deposited him on the settee and then turned and pulled her aunt into a big hug, not caring that she was sopping wet.

"Hello, Auntie, I'm so pleased to see you," said Lexey, releasing her and handing her the towel from the range rail. "This is Zak, and you'll also meet Jack and

Finn shortly. I'll explain in a moment, but first, where's Mum and Dad?"

"Ah," replied her aunt. "That's the problem. They are the other side of the lake still."

"How did you get here then?" asked Lexey in confusion.

"I rowed across the lake and then walked up," replied Aunt Jenny.

"Rowed? Walked? It's miles, Auntie!" said Lexey in astonishment.

"Don't I know it!" said Jenny. "My feet are killing me, and I'm wet through."

"Right, first things first," said Lexey, taking charge. "Sit by the range and I'll go and run you a hot bath. Zak — go and fetch your dad."

Lexey put the kettle onto the hotplate and then went upstairs to set the bath running. When she returned, Jack and Finn had joined them, and Aunt Jenny was just telling them that Lexey's parents were still on the other side of the lake in her car. She explained that she had rowed across in a dinghy which was now abandoned this side of the lake.

Jack and Finn set straight off to fetch Lexey's parents, taking Zak with them as he was bored and excited to see the dinghy row across the lake. Whilst Jenny went to soak in a hot bath, taking a mug of tea laced with whisky up with her, Lexey tried to keep herself busy while she waited, making soup and slicing bread, but soon gave up and just stood in the porch watching for Jack's car. The rain continued relentlessly, reducing visibility, but eventually she saw the car headlights cutting through the deluge, and she dashed out to greet her parents.

Her mum jumped out almost before the car stopped and gathered Lexey into her arms. Her dad wasn't far behind and put his arms around them both as the rain ran down their faces and mingled with their tears.

It wasn't until they got inside, that Lexey realised how thin and pale her dad was or how exhausted her mum looked, but there was far too much catching up to do to dwell on it just then. Aunt Jenny soon joined them, wrapped in a too-big dressing gown that had belonged to her late husband, and they all squashed around the kitchen table to demolish the simple meal Lexey had prepared.

"What I don't understand, is how you came to have a dinghy with you," said Jack.

"Well," explained Michael, "we got to York yesterday and went to the house. With all this rain, the water was starting to rise again, and it would probably have been just a few days until the street was evacuated again. After everything we'd been through, we made the decision we were not going to live there any more and we are going to put the house on the market, although goodness knows who would want it. I bought a second-hand trailer and we packed up what we could to bring with us. That included the escape dinghy, which we deflated and added to the trailer — never thought we'd have to re-inflate it and use it again so soon."

"When we got to the flooded valley, we thought we'd have to turn around and go back," Sarah took up the story, "but Jenny had the bright idea of rowing across and walking to the farm. I'm afraid it would have been too far for your dad to walk, so we stayed in the dry in the Land Rover on the other side."

"The boat had been left on this side of the lake," said Finn, "so Dad and I rowed over and picked up your parents and a few of their bits and pieces, and then rowed back to our car."

"So, the Land Rover is abandoned on the other side and the boat on this side still?" asked Lexey.

"Yes," said Jack, "but it's unlikely anyone will be about in this weather, and tomorrow I'll see if the Braithwaites can help with their tractor and trailer. We may have to leave the Land Rover for a while until the water has gone down, but we can bring everything out of it and then deflate the dinghy and bring it back.

"I've an idea," said Zak, "we could run a ferry service."

Everyone laughed, but Lexey took up the idea.

"Actually, that's not a bad idea," said Lexey. "It would be a real service for the community here and they could pay in goods, like we did at the market."

Everyone nodded, and Zak grinned, pleased with himself.

After such an exhausting day, everyone opted for an early night. The house was now full, and Lexey lay for a while and listened to the sounds of everyone moving around and then settling down. She mentally went around each room, like a sheep dog checking on its flock, and then lay back, contended that all were safety gathered in.

The next day, the rain had eased to a drizzle, and Stephen Braithwaite arrived with his tractor and trailer and then set off, with Jack and the boys following him in the car, to see if they could retrieve the Land Rover. Lexey showed her parents and aunt everything they had been doing on the farm and introduced them to Joy. Aunt Jenny agreed that it was the right decision to get rid of the pigs and was very interested in the new vegetable garden.

Over mugs of tea, Lexey filled them in on everything that had happened to her, leaving out the attempted assault and the fall down the mine shaft, as she didn't want to worry them. She did tell them about her shooting Finn, but instead of being cross with her, her aunt laughed.

"That will teach him to steal my eggs!" she said.

When Lexey told them about poor Zak being all alone and scared at the holiday cottage, Aunt Jenny was more sympathetic.

"Those poor boys!" she said. "You were absolutely right to let them move in here, and Jack too. If we'd have known you had good company, we'd have been less worried about you."

"I wasn't worried," said Michael. "I knew my Lexey could cope with anything."

He gave her a hug, and Lexey sank into his arms, feeling like a small child again.

"I'm very proud of you, darling," said her dad. "You've shown extraordinary resourcefulness and maturity."

"Thank you, Dad," said Lexey. "I feel like I've grown up ten years in as many weeks, but I'm so glad you are all here now, safe and well. I can relax and, well… just be a teenager again."

They grinned at each other, and then wandered over to the workshop to see what Jack had been working on.

"Wow," said Aunt Jenny, when she saw the sections of wind generator laid out around the workshop. "That is exactly what we need. I've lost track of the number of times I've lost power here."

"Don't I know it!" replied Lexey.

The sound of a vehicle horn brought them back into the yard in time to see the Land Rover being driven down the ramp from the tractor's high trailer. Jack's car then pulled up towing the trailer that had previously been attached to the Land Rover. The dinghy had been deflated and was piled on the trailer, but that wasn't what caught Lexey's attention. On the back seat of the car, her head against Finn's shoulder and fast asleep, was a young lady, her face shrouded in a mass of blonde hair. Lexey felt a stab of jealousy pierce her heart, shocking her at the depth of feelings she had for Finn.

Stephen was explaining to her mum and dad that due to the tractor's height and the higher-than-normal trailer, he was able to drive through the water and load the other trailer onto his and drive it back across, and then go back for the Land Rover. The water had come halfway up the sides of the Land Rover, but he didn't think any had got inside, but some of the stuff on the trailer had got a bit wet.

Lexey wasn't listening; she was watching Finn help the girl out of the car and all she wanted to know was who she was, where she had come from, and when she was going again.

Whilst the adults were thanking Stephen, Finn brought the girl over and introduced her to Lexey.

"Lexey, this is Sasha. We found her curled up asleep in the dinghy."

Up close the girl was bedraggled and pale but very pretty. Lexey tried hard to dampen down her feelings and say hello in a neutral tone.

"Hi, Sasha," she said. "Are you hungry?"

The girl nodded, and Lexey ushered her inside, but not before shooting Finn a look that he found hard to interpret.

Lexey quickly made Sasha a sandwich, which she wolfed done in just a few bites. She was obviously starving, and Lexey's heart softened a little and she turned to make her another sandwich, but when she turned back, the girl was curled up on the settee asleep. Finn gently tucked the wool throw around her, and then followed Lexey outside.

"Who is she, Finn?" she demanded, hands on her hips.

"I don't know," he said. "Apart from her name, she hasn't said anything."

"Oh, so you don't know her?" Lexey asked.

"No. We just found her when we tried to deflate the dinghy," he replied.

"How strange," replied Lexey, feeling a little relieved, and much more so when Finn pulled her close and gave her a quick kiss on the cheek when no one was looking.

Sasha woke up when Lexey was serving up lunch and joined them at the table.

"So, what were you doing out on the moors last night, Sasha?" asked Aunt Jenny, unable to wait any longer to solve the mystery of the girls asleep in the dinghy.

"I was running away," said Sasha in a quiet voice with an Eastern-European accent,

"Who from?" asked Michael.

"From the farm," said Sasha, looking down at her hands.

"What farm?" asked Jenny.

"I don't know where it is," replied Sasha, with a shrug of her shoulders. "It was dark when I was taken there, and dark when I escaped. I have been walking for days and got very lost on the moors in the rain, so I don't know where it is."

"You poor girl," said Sarah, putting her arm around Sasha's thin shoulders. "But why did you have to run away?"

"I was kept there to work. Kept locked in a room when not in the fields. Fed very little…"

"That's appalling!" cried Jenny, "Modern slavery. We need to ring the police!"

"No, please, no police!" cried Sasha, jumping up and knocking over a glass of water.

"Why ever not?" asked Michael, gently.

"Because I should not be here. I have no papers!" replied Sasha, backing towards the door.

"It's okay, Sasha," said Finn, taking her hand and leading her back to the table. "We won't contact the police, will we, Dad?"

The adults exchanged looks.

"Were there any other people kept there, Sasha?" he asked gently.

"No, just me," she replied. "There were others, but they went."

"Where did they go, Sasha?" asked Michael, looking very concerned.

"I don't know. They did not tell me. Please, can I stay here where I am safe?" asked Sasha, tears pooling in her eyes.

"Of course, you can stay here for a few days whilst we sort this out," said Jenny. "Finn can move in with

Zak — I think I have a camp bed somewhere — and you can have Finn's bed."

"Thank you, I'd like that," said Sasha, smiling sweetly from under eyelashes at Finn, who Lexey noticed was still holding Sasha's hand.

Lexey, who was mopping up the spilt water and not saying anything, also noticed how smooth Sasha's hands were, with neatly manicured fingernails. Not the hands of a farm worker....

Chapter Twenty

Over the next few days, the larger community at the farm settled into a rhythm; Zak fed the chickens, Michael looked after the other animals and attended to any small jobs around the farm and Jenny tended the established vegetable garden or helped Jack in the workshop. Sarah and Lexey seemed to be doing most of the cooking and housework, which, with the house full, was a lot more work than previously.

Whenever she could, Lexey worked on the new vegetable garden. Sometimes Finn worked alongside her, but too often whenever Lexey was free, Finn was nowhere about and she worked alone, struggling with hefting big stones into place to form the raised beds. She knew she should go and find someone to help her, but she channelled her frustration into moving stones, which left her exhausted but calmer by the time the family gathered in the kitchen each evening.

Sasha seemed to sleep in until midday every day, but after all she had been through, they were giving her a lot of leeway. Lexey wasn't sure what Sasha did the rest of the day, but she often heard her and Finn laughing together, and in the evenings, Sasha kept close to his side. Lexey tried her best to like Sasha but somehow couldn't shake off the bad feeling she got from her.

She told herself off for being uncharitable and admitted to herself that it was mainly jealousy that was colouring her feelings towards the poor girl. Finn was free to choose who he wanted — one little kiss didn't make him hers!

At the start of the second week, Lexey got a surprise that lifted her spirits when Seth Armstrong turned up with a captured swarm of bees for her. He brought with him a second-hand hat and veil, a beekeeper's smoker and a hive tool to get her started. Seth advised her to wear a thick long-sleeved top, long trousers, and tuck her trousers into wellington boots.

"Have you an old sheet we can use, please, Lexey?" he asked, and Lexey, somewhat surprised at this request, went to find one.

She watched as Seth secured one end of the sheet just below the hive entrance and then stretched the sheet to the ground, securing it with stones to form a ramp, before spreading out the rest on the grass. He put on his hat and veil, instructing Lexey to do the same, checking that she had draped it correctly, before he poured the bees onto the sheet. Some of the bees sort of knelt forward, sticking their bottoms in the air, flapping their wings but not flying.

"What are they doing?" asked Lexey

"They are releasing an orientation scent which they are fanning towards the entrance, to guide the other bees," said Seth.

As Lexey watched in fascination, the rest of the bees scrambled up the sheet and into the hive. Before long, none were left on the sheet, and bees were already flying in and out of the entrance.

"You'll get good honey here," said Seth, nodding toward the flower meadow where most of the bees were already heading. "You'll need to feed them a little sugar syrup through the hive-top feeder until they get going, up until you get half a dozen frames filled, I would suggest."

Lexey nodded, although she didn't have much of an idea what he was talking about, but over a mug of tea, Seth explained to her the basics, and agreed to be her mentor as she learnt more. After she had waved Seth off, she went to find Finn, excited to tell him that his hive was now full of bees. She found him in the barn with Sasha. Lexey didn't know what they were doing there together, but Sasha flashed her a triumphant smile, whilst Finn just looked guilty.

Lexey turned on her heel to leave without saying anything, but then realised that Sasha was wearing one of her favourite dresses.

"Hey, isn't that my dress?" she asked Sasha.

"Yeah, didn't think you'd mind me borrowing it as you never wear dresses," said Sasha with a nonchalant shrug.

"Well, you might have asked first!" said Lexey. "I don't wear dresses because I'm working on the farm, Sasha, and there is plenty for you to do too if you wouldn't mind lending a hand. But not in my dress — I was saving that for a special occasion, so please change out of it now, and I'll find you some trousers you can work in."

As Lexey strode out of the barn, trying to keep her temper, she could hear Sasha moaning to Finn about 'after everything she had been through, you'd think that lending her a dress wasn't too much to ask'. Lexey just kept going, not wanting to hear Finn's response.

Lexey went up to her bedroom and found the wardrobe door had been left open and a couple of items were on the floor where they had been knocked off their hangers. As she hung them up again, she could see other empty hangers where Sasha had evidently helped herself, and Lexey felt her blood boil. She would never have helped herself to someone else's things without asking, but maybe Sasha had been brought up differently. Lexey realised that they still knew very little about her and resolved to find out more over supper that evening.

Lexey was just leaving her room with a pair of old trousers and a faded T-shirt she was going to give to Sasha to work in, when something caught her eye and made her stop in her tracks. The corner of an old suitcase was peeking out from under the bed. Lexey knew there was nothing of financial value in the suitcase, it was just old school reports, photographs and other family memorabilia, but it had been tucked right under the bed and now it wasn't. But that wasn't what worried Lexey, it was what else she had been keeping under the bed she was concerned about.

Lexey got down on her hands and knees and lifted the edge of the quilt and peered beneath the bed, but it was gone — the loaded shotgun had disappeared.

Lexey raced into Sasha's room and searched it thoroughly but found no trace of the gun. She did find some of her aunt's jewellery tucked inside a sock and some suspicious packets of powder in the pocket of Sasha's jacket but left them exactly where she had found them as evidence. Retrieving the green tasselled key from her aunt's bedroom, Lexey went to check on the gun cabinet to see if perhaps her aunt had returned the gun to it, but two places in the rack remained empty. With her heart hammering, Lexey went to check the broom cupboard in the hall and was relieved to find that the second gun was still there.

Not sure what to do, Lexey went in search of her dad and found him with Jack in the workshop, helping him weld together sections of the turbine's tower. Lexey waited impatiently until they had finished and then closed the door before quietly explaining what she had found, or rather not found.

There was a moment's silence, and then Jack spoke.

"I thought something was not right about that girl's story," he said, "which is why I asked Finn to stay close to her."

Lexey's mouth fell open, and despite the seriousness of the situation, she felt a wave of relief wash over her.

"I spoke to the Braithwaites and we went through every farm within two to three days walk of where we found her, and not one of them could have been the set-up she described," said Jack.

"What's her game then?" asked Michael.

"I don't know, but now's the time to find out," said Jack with determination.

The three of them marched into the barn and found Sasha and Finn playing cards on a bale of straw.

"Hi, Dad," said Finn, looked from one to the other. Lexey realised how pale and unhappy Finn looked, and realised he must have been under strain too, playing a part at his dad's request.

"I want a word with you, young lady," said Jack, ignoring his son and looking directly at Sasha.

"Yeah?" said Sasha, looking all innocent. "How can I help you, Jack," she said sweetly.

"I want to know exactly what you are up to, but more importantly, where the gun is?" said Jack, advancing on her.

Sasha jumped up and backed away until she reached the straw bales stacked high against the far wall. Lexey had stopped just inside the barn door and from that angle could see Sasha feeling behind herself, her hand disappearing into a gap between two stacks.

"This gun, Jack?" Sasha said, pulling it out of its hiding place. All traces of her Eastern-European accent had gone, and, standing there arrogantly, tossing the gun casually from hands to hand, she seemed to be a completely different person.

"Give me that!" said Jack authoritatively, advancing slowly towards her with his hand out.

Sasha just grinned and raised the gun until it was pointing directly at his chest.

"Put it down, Sasha," shouted Finn, rushing toward her and placing himself between his dad and the gun. "Come on, Sasha, don't be stupid," he said. "I thought we were friends. Give me the gun and I'm sure we can sort this all out."

"Friends?" spat out Sasha. "God, you don't know how annoying you are, hanging around me like a dog on heat. I've just been stringing you along because it amused me to make your girlfriend jealous!"

Lexey was too scared for Finn and Jack's safety to feel relief. She tried to sneak out to get help, but Sasha saw her.

"Stay where you are, you stuck up cow, or I'll shoot your boyfriend. All of you, into the house. Now!" Sasha commanded, waving the gun around.

Hands in the air, the four of them filed into the house. Sarah and Jenny were in the kitchen and turned in surprise as they burst through the door.

"What the—" said Sarah before Sasha came into the kitchen and realisation dawned.

"Oh, Sasha," she said sadly. "We took you in, fed you, looked after you... surely we can sort out whatever is wrong without all this?"

"Shut up, you stupid old woman," said Sasha. "Fed me! Vegetarian rubbish and wholemeal bread. Don't know how I ate it without throwing up!"

"What is it you want, Sasha, if that's even your name?" said Michael, putting his arm around his wife who was visible shaking.

"Of course, it's not my name," said 'Sasha', in a parody of her previous accent. "What do I want? Everything you've got that's worth taking! I've already got the jewellery I was sent for, but you must have more. So, money, watches — put them all on the table."

Lexey gasped, realising 'Sasha' must have been sent by Shaun, the ponytailed farmhand who had tried to assault her. She remembered she had pulled the same gun on him, taking it from under her bed, which would be how Sasha knew it was there. Her thoughts turned to the other loaded gun which was hidden in the hall. Could she get to it? She looked around the room, at everyone she held dear, and knew she mustn't do anything to put them in danger. Then she realised that someone was missing. Where was Zak?

Her blood ran cold, imagining what could happen if Zak, clumsy on his crutches, suddenly burst unsuspecting into the room. Sasha hadn't noticed he was missing, probably because she had never taken any notice of him before.

"Come on, I haven't got all day," shouted Sasha, waving the gun around. "I'm being picked up this evening, and believe me, they will happily slit your throats, if I tell them you have been holding out on us"

Jack took off his watch and laid it on the table, along with his wallet, and then Michael followed suit.

Sasha pointed the gun at Sarah.

"Your rings," she demanded.

"No," said Sarah, defiantly. "I've not taken them off in twenty years of marriage, and I'm not taking them off now!"

"You will if you want to remain a wife and not a widow," said Sasha coldly, aiming the gun at Michael.

Sarah gave a sob and started to tug at the rings on her finger, but they were stuck fast.

Whilst everyone was distracted, Lexey watched Zak hobble across the yard and tried to catch his attention without being seen by Sasha, but Zak was oblivious. Lexey knew she had to do something, and fast.

"There is some oil in the hall cupboard," she said. "If I put some on Mum's finger, it will ease the rings off.

"Okay," said Sasha, moving towards the door, "you get it, but I can see you from here, so if you try anything funny, I'll shoot your father."

Lexey moved into the hall, her heart thudding in her chest, and opened the broom cupboard door. Then several things happened almost at once. Zak threw the back door open with a bang, a gun went off with a much louder bang and then the air was full of screams and shattering glass.

Chapter Twenty-One

When Sasha's gun went off, the shot shattered the hall window, terrifying poor Zak who screamed loudly. He was badly shaken but otherwise unhurt, one piece of shot and some glass fragments having embedded in his cast, but thankfully not reaching his leg beneath.

In the confusion, Lexey had immediately pulled the second gun from the cupboard and held it steady on Sasha until she was overpowered by Jack and Finn. They tied her to a kitchen chair until the police arrived, two cars screaming down the road with blue lights flashing, an alien sight bright against the misty moors. An ambulance had automatically been dispatched, but apart from treating Zak for shock, it was not needed. Sasha was bundled into a police car and taken away under arrest, disappearing quickly along with the ambulance into the mist.

The second police team searched Sasha's room and took away the drugs, the guns and Aunt Jenny's jewellery, promising to return the guns and jewellery as soon as possible. They found a list of other local properties in Sasha's bag, and a big wad of money tied up with an elastic band.

Lexey told the police about her suspicion that Sasha was in league with Shaun and his partner, and about Shaun's assault on her weeks before. Her mum and dad were shocked, dismayed that Lexey had been through that all alone and had not told them.

The police explained that they had been after the pair for a long time for running a 'County Lines' drug gang, and suspected that Sasha was one of their runners, bringing in drug supplies. Theft and other petty crime had followed the pair as they moved north, expanding their empire into rural areas by getting casual work on farms whilst they sussed out the competition, customers and potential victims.

In anticipation of the pair coming back that evening for Sasha as planned, the second police car was driven into the barn out of sight, and armed police took up positions in hiding to wait.

Sarah made everyone tea, and they sat around the kitchen clutching their mugs, hoping the warmth would take away the chill that had settled on them all. Jenny and Jack sat on the settee, Jack with both arms around Zak, rocking him gently. At the kitchen table Sarah and Michael sat holding hands and Finn sat with his arm around Lexey. Lexey rested her head against his shoulder and felt the tension of the last few days start to drain away.

"What I can't understand," said Michael, "is how Sasha came to be in the dinghy, and so became the cuckoo in our nest?"

"You know when we went to pick you up from the other side of the lake?" asked Finn.

"Yes?" replied Michael.

"Well, when we were rowing across to get you, I saw a black pick-up truck drive up and stop next to the car, before turning around and driving back the way they came," said Finn.

"Zak, you were still in the car," said Jack, "did they speak to you?"

Zak nodded his head.

"What did they say to you Zak," Jack asked him gently.

"They asked me where we were from and I told them we were from the farm here," muttered Zak, a little shamefacedly. "They asked if we were going to take the dinghy away or run a ferry service — that's where I got the idea from — it wasn't really my idea at all. It's my fault she came here, isn't it?"

Zak burst into tears, and Jack comforted him.

"It's okay, Zak, none of this is your fault. They are just bad people."

"They must have dropped Sasha off a little higher up the moors and instructed her to wait in the dinghy overnight in order that she could get into our house," said Lexey. "She didn't need to fake being wet, tired and hungry after a night in an open dinghy in the pouring rain."

Just then one of the policemen came into the kitchen. "Sorry to disturb you, but we've just had a message that a black pickup has been seen heading this way," he said. "We need you all to stay in the kitchen, pull the curtains and stay away from the windows."

Finn closed the curtains and they all sat in silence, trying to hear what was going on outside. They heard a vehicle pull up and someone try the front door; then there was a lot of shouting, running feet, a scuffle and then... silence. It was an agonising fifteen minutes later before the policeman returned and told them that the suspects had been apprehended and all was safe. The police would need to come back tomorrow and take statements etcetera, but other than that they were free to carry on as normal.

They all looked at each other and then burst out laughing. It was partly the relief, and partly that nothing had been 'normal' for a long time. Here they were, two unrelated families in one house, city dwellers and country folk mixed together, the whole world changing rapidly in order that human beings could survive in a climate that was becoming increasingly hostile.

They weren't sure what *was* normal any more, but they knew that, together, they could make a good life that would be their 'normal'.

Chapter Twenty-Two
New Helmsley District,
North Yorkshire Moors, 2055

"Hurry up, Saffron, time to get ready," shouted Lexey.

"Aw, Mum, do I have to?" replied Saffron, coming in reluctantly from playing in the farmyard, her face and knees streaked with dirt and her curly dark hair a tangled mess.

"Yes, you do, and you'll need to get washed and comb your hair before you put your dress on," said Lexey, trying to hide a smile as her tomboy daughter stomped upstairs in a sulk.

"I don't know, Finn," said Lexey, "any other little girl would be delighted to be a bridesmaid. Daisy is *so* excited and has been dressed and ready for over an hour!"

"Yes, but I wouldn't change Saffie for any other little girl, would you?" he replied.

"No," replied Lexey. "She's so different from Daisy, isn't she?

"She's more like you, strong and independent, I think," replied Finn, coming up and encircling her in his arms.

"Really?" said Lexey surprised, never having thought of herself in that way.

"Really," replied Finn, "and I wouldn't change you either."

With both children out of the room, Finn took the opportunity to kiss Lexey deeply.

"Have I told you today that I love you, Mrs O'Connell?" he asked a long moment later, smoothing a stray strand of hair off her face.

"Yes, but you can tell me again," she said with a smile, before a wail from Saffron's room made her reluctantly leave the haven of his arms.

It was nearly ten years since they got married, but the passion they felt for each other hadn't dimmed at all; however, with two children under eight, the farm and her civic duties, finding time to be alone was increasingly difficult. Still, it was a good life, and today was a special day, one the whole community were coming together to celebrate.

Having tamed Saffron's hair and persuaded her into her new shoes, Lexey checked her own reflection in the mirror. At just over thirty, and after two children, she wasn't quite as slim as she used to be, but Finn said the curves suited her, and if he was happy with her, she wasn't going to stress about it. The mainly outdoor life kept her face and arms tanned and put fairer streaks into her shoulder-length hair and she was pleased with the somewhat haphazard updo she had constructed.

Picking up a beautiful, locally-made, deep purple wool shawl, she went to corral the children into the car for the short trip to the Hub. Finn, as the best man, had already set off with the groom in the horse drawn buggy.

The Moorland Hub, a purpose-built building in the middle of the moors, was, as the name suggested, the hub of their community. It served as a medical centre, a nursery school, a sports centre, an entertainment venue, an indoor market and, as today, a venue for weddings and other celebrations. It was also the centre for local government, and Lexey, as the recently elected mayor of the district, spent many long hours there in meetings or just listening to residents' concerns. She had a weekly conference call with mayors from other districts, and a monthly call with the regional minister in York.

The almost constant rain in the twenties and thirties had started the process of flooding of all the low-lying areas of the country, but rapidly rising sea levels due to melting polar ice caps in the thirties and forties had accelerated the process. Now Britain was a patchwork of islands, and most, like her own district, were almost self-sufficient and semi-autonomous.

Although there was still plenty of manufacturing in the previously industrial parts of the world, clean energy sources and careful environmental management had stopped global warming at two degrees. The United British Islands still had more than their fair share of rain, but the weather was more settled than it had been when Lexey was growing up, and today was a glorious day of clear spring sunshine with just a little breeze to stop the heat being overpowering.

Arriving at the Hub, Lexey was greeted warmly by friends and neighbours, who oohed and aahed over the girls, despite Saffron's scowls. Five-year-old Daisy looked immaculate, her long golden-brown hair as smooth as silk, her white socks pulled up and her shoes shiny. By contrast, seven-year-old Saffron's lilac hair ribbon was already undone, one sock was up and the other down, and somehow in the last half hour she had managed to scuff her new shoes. Lexey sighed and followed the girls into the circular central hall of the Hub.

The room looked beautiful with purple and lilac ribbons raining down from the light filled cupola, and Lexey's beeswax candles burning brightly and filling the hall with the scent of honey. Most of the guests were wearing something in tones of purple and all the men had a sprig of heather in their buttonholes reflecting the moorland theme. Finn was already in the centre of the hall with the nervous groom, and he turned and blew her a kiss. She blew one back, thinking how handsome he looked, and those that saw it smiled, remembering Lexey and Finn's own wedding, the first in the then newly constructed Hub.

Having satisfied herself everything was ready, Lexey took the girls back outside to look out for the bride and they jumped up and down with excitement as the Braithwaites' tractor, bedecked in purple ribbons, lumbered down the road towards them. Stephen, although nearly eighty, was driving, and his granddaughter, Amy, was perched serenely besides him, her long lilac dress blowing out behind her.

Lexey helped her alight and gave her a quick hug, and, having given the girls strict instructions on their duties in attending the bride, she and Stephen took their seats in the hall next to Marie, Jenny, Jack and her parents. The music started, and everyone turned to watch as a radiant Amy floated in, Saffron and Daisy holding her train and, for once, behaving impeccably. Zak turned to see his beautiful bride walking towards him at last, and stood transfixed, his face lit up with love.

Zak had first asked Amy to marry him on the evening of Finn and Lexey's wedding, when he was only sixteen. She had laughed, thinking he was joking, but he had asked her every year since on the same day. It had taken her almost another ten years to say yes, but later, as they took the first dance, looking deeply into each other's eyes, everyone could see that the wait had been worth it.

The celebration lasted well into the night, but before it finished Finn and Lexey had to leave to take the sleepy girls home. As they drove away, Lexey looked back at the Hub, light and music streaming from it out across the dark moors. She thought it looked like a spaceship and wondered idly what aliens would think if they were looking down on this world of interconnected islands which must look like cells in a beehive.

Once the girls were safely tucked up, Finn and Lexey enjoyed a rare moment of peace together, holding hands as they rocked gently in the chairs on the porch. The chairs had been Finn's first project during his woodworking apprenticeship many years ago, and although they were not perfect, they were one of Lexey's most treasured possessions. Finn had also built the wrap-around porch where the family gathered most evenings to watch the sunset and talk about their day.

The old farmhouse, and the family within it, had evolved constantly over the years, but built on solid foundations it remained strong. Lexey poured them both a glass of her honey mead and they talked and laughed about the day, whilst they looked out over the farm bathed in moonlight. They still kept chickens, goats and several ponies, but the farm was mainly dedicated to vegetable production and beekeeping. Wind turbines and banks of solar panels kept them, and the village that had sprung up around the farm, supplied with electricity.

As people had been forced to make their homes on the higher ground of the moors, Lexey had been very active in ensuring that everything that was built, and every local occupation, was carbon neutral and added to the overall community wellbeing. It was this campaigning that had led to her being voted, overwhelmingly, to be the district's mayor, an accolade

Finn was very proud of but that Lexey just took in her stride.

The first house built had been for Lexey's parents, Michael and Sarah. Michael's health had never fully recovered, and they decided a house all on one level would be a good idea as they got older. The house was built of hay bales, which were super-insulating, and had a turf roof, so it blended well into the landscape. It became the prototype of the inexpensive carbon neutral houses to follow, each with a plot of land big enough to grow vegetables and keep a few chickens so that each household could be self-sufficient.

Zak had been building and refining his home for the last five years, but had remained living at the farm, waiting until Amy said 'yes' before they moved into the house, together. Tonight, they would return to the house that had been waiting for them, and Lexey smiled, thinking how lovely it had looked when she'd left it ready that morning, full of flowers and dozens of candles waiting to be lit.

Before long Aunt Jenny and Jack returned and joined them for a little while on the porch, chatting about the day before retiring to bed. Theirs had been a slow burning love story, one no one really commented on; they were just 'Jack and Jenny' as if that had always been the case. Jack had just moved into Jenny's bedroom one night around the time of Lexey and Finn's wedding and had remained there ever since.

Before going to bed, Lexey wandered over to the old beehive in the garden to tell the bees about the happy day. It was an ancient tradition that Lexey kept up, not out of superstition, but because it was a way of clearing her mind each day. Returning to the farmhouse and snuggled up to a sleeping Finn, Lexey smiled, thinking how good life was now. It hadn't always been so, and in the past the bees had regularly been informed of some scary situations.

In the early years they had had to fortify the farm against those that wanted to take away everything they had worked for. As people moved in large numbers to higher ground, for a period everything was pretty lawless, every man for himself as people tried to survive in this new world. Eventually a new civilisation started to form, with each district doing what the land and local heritage made it best suited for, and the people who shared those skills and values stayed there.

The moorland community were mainly farmers and had voted against the building of a bridge across the lake as that gave them a little bit of separation from others who may not respect the land like they did. As a teenager, Zak had run a ferry service, initially using the old dinghy for foot passengers only, but eventually funds were raised for a chain ferry that could take vehicles across. Teenager Joel Lex now ran the ferry, under Zak's supervision, as Zak mainly helped Finn in his woodworking business, when he wasn't helping Jenny on the farm.

Lexey also helped on the farm, but spent a lot of time managing her bees, with hives spread across the moors and specialising in heather honey. Bottling the honey and making beeswax candles and mead was a cottage industry employing lots of local people, especially older people, or people with disabilities, who wanted a little light work. Just before she drifted off to sleep, Lexey said a silent thank you to Seth Armstrong, now long gone, for all his help and patient tuition whilst she was learning the craft of beekeeping.

Chapter Twenty-Three

Morning came too soon, the alarm's shrill call pulling Lexey from a dream where she was a child again in York. In her dream the ancient city of York was intact, its medieval streets bustling with tourists, the little shops full of wonderful food, clothes and gifts. Very little of York now remained above water, the towers of the minster and the many other ancient church spires were fingers pointing accusingly at the heavens from the middle of the vast lake that was once the Vale of York.

Knowing that she had a busy day ahead of her, Lexey reluctantly got straight out of bed and then stood under a hot shower to wake herself up. Finn brought her a cup of tea before he too got a quick shower, knowing he also hadn't much time before he needed to hustle Daisy off to school at the Hub. Saffron's lessons were streamed straight to her home, and Lexey was relying on Jenny to get her up and at her virtual desk on time for registration.

Lexey chatted to Joel Lex as she crossed on the ferry, then drove into Helmsley, ready to oversee the paying of the quarterly tithes to the government. Ten percent of all the food and goods produced in each district was collected each quarter for regional storehouses. Individuals could order anything they wanted for delivery by drone from these central stores, paying with credits earned if they submitted more than the mandatory ten percent.

Lexey, as mayor, could have left it to an assistant to oversee the handover of the tithes and any additional goods to the government officers. However, knowing how hard her people worked, she liked to oversee it herself, making sure everything was properly accounted for and all additional credits logged correctly. She arrived in Helmsley just as the convoy of government trucks came over the new bridge into the town. Half the original town had been lost to the water, but All Saints Church, built on deep ancient foundations on a slight rise, had survived intact. The commercial centre of New Helmsley was now on higher ground in the former parkland of Duncombe Park and the historic Duncombe Park House had been converted into the Helmsley Hub.

Lexey headed for the huge tents erected outside the Hub which contained her district's tithes and greeted the government inspector warmly, having met him several times before. This time of year, the accounting wasn't too bad, as most arable crops had yet to be harvested, and they would be paid in one bulk contribution in the autumn.

Lexey went through the ledgers with the inspector as his men loaded the trucks. She was pleased to record a lot of honey, mead and beeswax candles as additional goods which would be credited to her account. Fresh goods, like eggs, meat and vegetables, were delivered weekly by drone to the government storehouses, so for them she just needed to double check that the inspector's records matched her own.

Lexey was relieved that the inspector had brought her new supplies for the Moorland Hub's medical centre. All but the most complex surgery could be undertaken by a surgeon operating a surgical robot remotely, but Lexey needed to ensure that any consumables for the remote diagnostic unit and the surgical robot were always available for when they were needed.

Patients entering the diagnostic unit would input details of their problem and then pick up a sterile straw and fit it into the diagnostic machine to give a sample of breath. This was analysed, and usually a diagnosis would be given almost immediately and then prescriptions delivered by drone direct to the patient. Occasionally, a face-to-face consultation was needed via the internet, and very occasionally surgery. Each district had several qualified nurses who would attend to oversee the patient's care during surgery or would help transfer the patient to a regional hospital by medical drone should the condition be more serious.

Her duties eventually concluded, Lexey visited the open-air market and swapped honey, eggs, bread and vegetables for some second-hand machinery parts that Jack had asked her to try and get, and some treats for the girls. She dithered about bartering for a pretty dress for

Daisy, but knew Saffron wouldn't want one, so instead she bought the girls new colouring pencils and some chocolate buttons. She got a couple of extra packets of chocolate for Finn, otherwise the girls' stash wouldn't be safe.

By the time Lexey caught the ferry back home it was almost dark, and as she drove the unlit narrow road over the moors, a bright green aurora started to dance around the car. It was a little while since there had been one, and Lexey pulled over and walked across to the viewpoint to watch it. She climbed up the rocks and sat cross-legged on the top as waves of green and pink danced across the dark moors and were mirrored in the lake far below.

Lexey felt like the show was being put on just for her, and suddenly remembered sitting here as a teenager, during a time when phones and the internet weren't working, and she had no way of contacting her family. She remembered how utterly alone she had felt then, completely cut off from all she knew and loved, adrift in a world that she didn't understand. Lexey briefly hoped that the solar flares that created the lights wouldn't take out electronic communications as they had back then, and then realised that wouldn't matter, her community were strong enough to cope.

She had learnt over the years that the human race would always find a way to survive, even when everything seemed stacked against them. She had learnt that everyone is capable of far more than they think they are, and the more pressure that is heaped upon you, the stronger you grow to withstand it.

Lexey had learnt the moods of the moorland and farmland and the skills she needed to work with it, not against it. Crops were rotated and fields left fallow for a season to reduce the leaching of soil nutrients. Weeds high in nitrogen were allowed to grow and then used as 'green manure', ploughed back into the soil to improve it, rather than using chemical fertilisers.

Life now was both very simple and very complex, Lexey mused. She remembered studying medieval history a long time ago at school, learning about small homesteads grouped into communities growing what they ate and bartering for things they couldn't produce themselves. Most of the world had gone back to a very similar way of life, but, at the same time, used whatever modern technology was developed to support this simple way of life without detracting from it. Technology was now the servant, not the master, and Lexey was glad that her daughters would grow up in a real world that didn't revolve constantly around a screen or vacuous 'celebrities'.

Lexey remained where she was as the night grew cool around her, mesmerised by the majesty and mystery around her. Here on the moors, she had found her place in the universe.

Standing and stretching as the lights faded, she eventually made her way back to the farm, to her children and to the man she loved. She was home.

THE END